THROUGH DEAD EYES

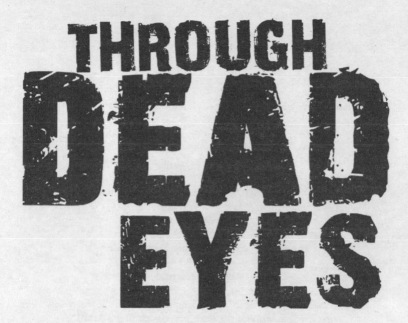

THROUGH DEAD EYES

CHRIS PRIESTLEY

BLOOMSBURY

LONDON NEW DELHI NEW YORK SYDNEY

Bloomsbury Publishing, London, New Delhi, New York and Sydney

First published in Great Britain in March 2013 by
Bloomsbury Publishing Plc
50 Bedford Square, London WC1B 3DP

This paperback edition published in March 2014

A CIP catalogue record for this book is
available from the British Library

ISBN 978 1 4088 1107 8

Typeset by Hewer Text UK Ltd, Edinburgh
Printed and bound in Great Britain by CPI
Group (UK) Ltd, Croydon CR0 4YY

1 3 5 7 9 10 8 6 4 2

www.bloomsbury.com
www.chrispriestleybooks.com

For Hannah
(*who isn't anything like Hanna*)

I

The plane dipped out of dazzling sunshine into a grey mass of cloud. Beads of rainwater scurried diagonally down the glass, trembling as they did so. The wing tip was obscured and revealed and obscured once again in rapid succession as the plane descended through the formless murk of cloud, until a darkened landscape was laid out beneath them.

Alex rubbed his eyes, peering at the motorway that snaked below the wing's edge, bejewelled with twinkling headlights. It was ten o'clock in the morning, but it seemed the night had never fully let go of its grip on the day.

The tyres smacked the runway. The plane shook and juddered, roaring as it slowed down, and then began to taxi to the terminal. The pilot welcomed them – in Dutch and English – to Schiphol airport and to Amsterdam. In his head Alex had pronounced it *Skipol* – like school – and was surprised that it was actually Shipol. Alex's father turned to him and smiled.

'Well,' he said, 'Amsterdam awaits.'

Alex nodded and stretched his legs, yawning, and slipped a bookmark into his book before closing it. The plane came to a halt. The passengers immediately and noisily began to get their things from the overhead lockers and switch on their mobile phones.

The man sitting next to Alex's father unbuckled his seat belt and stood up to get his bag. There was a huge sweat stain in the shape of Africa under his armpit.

'I'd better check to see if there are any messages from Saskia . . .' said Alex's father.

Saskia worked for his father's publishers. He was an expert on the Second World War and his recent book about occupied Amsterdam had become a bestseller in Holland as well as in England.

'She's meeting us at the gate.' His father put his phone in his jacket pocket.

Alex followed his father out into the aisle, grabbed his bag and shuffled towards the exit at the front of the plane.

'Goodbye,' said the stewardess at the door with a mechanical smile. 'Enjoy your stay.'

It was March and spring was slow in coming. A dank breeze blew in through the open door as they stepped out into the rain. The metal staircase looked slippery and Alex gripped tightly to the cold, wet handrail. The air was filled with the angry roar of aircraft engines.

Men in fluorescent yellow jackets and ear defenders stood waiting on the wet tarmac as the passengers hurried to the shelter of the arrivals building.

Alex and his father joined the long and shapeless queue at passport control.

Alex's father grabbed his arm. 'Try to cheer up a bit, Alex, for goodness' sake.'

Alex sighed loudly.

'Stop wallowing,' said his father. 'You're never going to make anything better by moping about.'

Alex shrugged. His father scowled and turned back to the queue.

Alex took out his iPod, put the earbuds in and scrolled down to shuffle. The opening notes of 'Seven Nation Army' started up. The White Stripes always reminded Alex of his mother. She hated them. She used to yell at him to turn it down when he was playing them in his bedroom. It was nearly a year since she had moved out, but Alex still couldn't listen to them without thinking of her. He flicked to the next song and tried to put her out of his mind.

The sullen official at passport control looked at the photo of Alex and then at him, then back to the photo. He handed the passports back with a nod, and Alex and his father continued on their way, walking through a doorway into the arrivals hall.

A small crowd of people, some holding boards with names on, were waiting for passengers on the other side of a low barrier. A woman in her forties with shoulder-length blonde hair was waving at them. Alex recognised her from the photo his father had stuck to the fridge door at home.

'Jeremy!' she called.

The name sounded so different in her accent that it took Alex a couple of seconds to realise it was his father's name.

'Saskia!' replied Alex's father.

The woman moved through the crowd to meet them at the end of the barrier. Alex's father put his bag down and they embraced.

'It's so lovely to see you again, Jeremy,' said Saskia. 'How was your flight?'

'It was fine. No hold-ups.'

'This is my daughter, Angelien,' said Saskia.

Alex hadn't noticed her until that point, but a tall, thin girl stepped forward. She wore tight skinny jeans and a silver puffa jacket with a white-fur-trimmed hood. Her hands were thrust deep into the pockets of the jacket, which was open, revealing a

T-shirt with a picture of the full moon, blue against a square of black night.

She was about twenty, Alex guessed. She was blonde, like her mother, though her hair was longer. Her face was pale and round, and serious despite her smile.

'Nice to meet you, Angelien,' said Alex's father. His father kissed her on both cheeks. 'You're studying history, I hear.'

Angelien nodded. 'I'm working on my doctorate.'

'It must be in the blood,' said Saskia. She turned towards Alex. 'And this must be your son,' said Saskia. 'You look just like your father when he was a student. When we were at Oxford, you know? He was very good looking. Very sexy.'

Alex blushed and looked away. Angelien rolled her eyes behind Saskia's back.

'Mother!'

Alex laughed.

Saskia raised an eyebrow and turned to look at her daughter.

'Do you see?' said Saskia with a smile. 'They are ganging up on us already. Come – let's get you to your hotel. The car's over here.'

Angelien linked arms with her mother and they headed towards the car park, Alex and his father following behind.

They put their bags in the boot of the black Volvo and Alex's father got in the front seat beside Saskia. Angelien sat in the back with Alex, her face hidden by the fur trim of her hood.

'So,' said Saskia as she started up the car. 'This is your first time in Amsterdam, Alex?'

'Yes,' he replied.

'We'll have to make sure you enjoy it.' Saskia smiled at him in the rear-view mirror.

They left the car park and the indicator ticked as they headed swiftly out into the traffic.

'You are not here for so very long,' said Saskia, 'and there are so many things to see in Amsterdam. You will just have to come back another time, won't you?'

Saskia smiled at him again in the rear-view mirror. Angelien fired off a volley of Dutch.

'English please, darling,' said Saskia. 'It's rude to our guests.'

'I said watch the road and stop driving so goddam fast.'

Alex's father gave an embarrassed chuckle. Angelien looked at Alex and shook her head. Saskia and Alex's father started up a conversation. Alex tuned it out and stared out of the window.

A double-decker train rattled past them on the rail tracks that ran alongside the motorway. A canal wended its way nearby, reeds growing along the banks.

The motorway they drove along seemed just like the motorways in England – except they were driving on the wrong side of the road. The buildings they drove past looked mundanely familiar: a succession of tombstone-grey apartment blocks. They could almost have been driving through the outskirts of London. He had expected things to be more different.

It wasn't until they entered the centre of Amsterdam that the city started to look more like the photos his father had shown him before they left: rows of tall, thin houses whose walls rose up to gable tops that were stepped or decorated with swirls and scrolls. Instead of being straight, like a terraced street in London, the roofline was higgledy-piggledy, each house seeming to compete with the one next door.

'It's a beautiful city,' said Saskia. 'Although I am a little biased, of course. But I think you will love it.'

Alex glanced at Saskia's face in the rear-view mirror and looked out of the window again.

His father had said the trip would be a chance for them to spend some time together, although he was going to have to work some of the time.

The publishers were paying for Alex's father to come to Holland to talk to television people who were interested in screening a documentary to tie in with a new edition of his book. Alex's father had taken a great deal of time to explain just how important it all was.

Saskia was in charge of liaising with the television companies. His father called her an 'old friend from university', but Alex could tell they had been more than just friends back then.

Angelien had said nothing after her outburst. She seemed lost in her own thoughts and intent on ignoring Alex, who looked out at the view. Saskia was right – it was beautiful.

The city seemed to be squeezing in around them now, the roads narrower, the buildings taller and darker. Every now and again Alex would catch a glimpse of a long stretch of gloomy water as they drove over a bridge.

They slowed down and turned off the main road into a narrow road that ran alongside a canal. The car tyres rumbled along the cobbles and tramlines.

'Here we are,' said Saskia, putting the handbrake on noisily. 'It's a lovely hotel. You'll be very comfortable.'

Alex's father leaned over and kissed Saskia on the cheek. 'Thanks for sorting everything out this end,' he said and then opened the car door. Alex followed him out and they stood together on the pavement.

A cyclist sped past, large headphones on, singing along enthusiastically, his voice trembling comically as the wheels juddered over the cobbles.

'We'll book a restaurant for this evening,' said Saskia. 'Do you like Indonesian food?'

Alex's father looked at him and Alex shrugged. He had never had Indonesian food. How was he supposed to know if he liked it or not?

His father frowned.

Alex hunched his shoulders and shivered. He felt cold all of a sudden. He gazed at the canal. It was so black it could have been filled with oil.

'Indonesian would be great,' he heard his father say.

Alex felt the hairs on the back of his neck stand up. He had the strongest feeling that someone was watching him. He turned and looked up at the hotel, his eyes drawn to a specific window, but the lights were out and he could see nothing there.

Alex turned back to Saskia's car. The darkened windows reflected the hotel above. Just for an instant, in the window he had been drawn to, he was sure he saw a face – a strange, pale face – looking back at him. But when he turned to look at the actual hotel, the window was as blank as before.

'See you at two,' his father said.

'Great! See you later,' said Saskia, before waving and driving away.

'Alex!' said his father. 'You could at least have said goodbye.'

But Alex was still staring at the hotel window, searching for any hint that there was someone there.

2

The lobby was small and modern and shiny but full of antique furniture. Old paintings and engravings in gilded frames were hung on the walls. Alex did not have much to compare it with, having stayed in very few hotels, but it looked expensive.

His father went to the reception counter and the manager, dressed smartly in a black suit and tie, smiled and looked for his name on the computer before giving him a key. Alex's father raised his eyebrows.

'A real key,' he said. 'I can't remember the last time I was given a real key in a hotel. I thought you'd all changed to those swipe cards.'

A large grandfather clock nearby chimed the hour.

'Yes,' said the manager. 'But our customers seem to like it. This one is for you, sir,' he said, handing a second key to Alex, the metal chilling the palm of his hand as he took hold of it.

'We have adjoining rooms,' explained his father. 'I thought you'd like that.'

Alex grinned. 'Cool,' he said.

He had never stayed in his own room before.

'Interesting key rings,' said Alex's father, turning his over in his hand. It was a silver lion's head, very worn and hollow at the neck and attached by a small chain to the key. 'Is that the handle from a walking stick?'

The manager nodded.

'Yes. My late wife would trawl the antiques market looking for anything suitable. She tried to pick objects that might have come from this type of house in the seventeenth century. A lot of the furniture you see around the hotel and the prints and paintings are things she bought. She said that the pieces spoke to her and she just had to buy them.'

The manager chuckled to himself.

'I wish some of the cheaper things had shouted a little louder.'

'What's yours, Alex?' asked his father.

'I don't know,' said Alex, looking at the disc of metal, with its coiled silver rim, sitting in the palm of his hand.

'Ah, yes,' said the manager. 'That is a brooch. Or at least it was. It would have held a cameo probably, but we only have the backing plate.'

The manager gave them the speech about what time breakfast was and where it was served, and then pointed to a man in a waistcoat standing nearby, and said that he would show them to their rooms.

'They are a little tricky to find for the first time, I'm afraid,' he said with a smile.

Alex and his father followed the porter past the small lift and up a narrow flight of stairs that curved back on itself sharply. They then walked along a corridor lined with old engravings of Amsterdam and through a fire door to climb an even narrower staircase that led to a small landing.

'Here we are, gentlemen,' the porter said.

The porter put a key in the lock of room forty-five and opened the door. He showed them where the bathroom was and how the television worked and how to control the air-conditioning.

'Some people have complained that the air-con is chilly in this room. But if you feel cold, just turn this. Any problems, let someone know at the desk.'

The porter walked over to another door and opened it, revealing an almost identical room on the other side.

'Wow,' said Alex, stepping through the open door. 'Is this my room?'

His father nodded.

Alex walked straight over to the window and looked at the view of the canal below.

'Will that be everything?' he heard the porter say next door. Alex put his bag on the floor. He had a double bed and there was a table and chairs. He noticed that there were flowers in a jug and a note leaning against it. He picked it up. It said, *Hope you enjoy your stay, love Saskia xxx*

Alex turned back to the window, which stretched almost floor to ceiling. It was still dingy outside and rain was falling steadily. The glass was a partial mirror reflecting Alex and the room behind him.

He looked at the buildings on the opposite side. They were similar to the one he was in: tall and thin with decorated gable tops. A line of trees partially obscured them, and cars were parked beneath those all along the canal.

Looking directly down, Alex could see the place where Saskia had dropped them off. This was the very room he had been looking up at; he was sure of it. Just as he realised this, the feeling of dread he had experienced returned with its previous force and startling suddenness.

Alex spun round, sure that someone was behind him. The room was empty. Empty. Definitely. He turned back to the window, but so strong was the feeling that someone was there he turned to look again.

There was nothing – nothing at all – to account for the sensation. Still, Alex felt so troubled by it that he found himself checking behind the bathroom door, despite feeling more than a little foolish for doing so.

Though he had confirmed that the room was empty, the feeling of disquiet obstinately refused to go away.

Alex returned to the window and peered out into the murk, hoping that the view of the world outside would calm his nerves. The hotel stood on a stretch of canal between two bridges and if Alex looked right and left he could just see both of them.

A couple went by below, arm in arm, hurrying to find shelter from the downpour. Their voices carried faintly through the air, muffled by the window glass. The woman laughed and looked up towards Alex and he ducked inside, embarrassed to be caught spying.

Alex turned round again. The room was empty and bright. It was conspicuously free of dark shadows or peculiarities of any kind. And yet Alex could feel his heartbeat speeding. The faintest of breezes, almost imperceptible, moved the hairs on his arms as though someone had crept past him unseen. The connecting door suddenly opened and Alex flinched.

'Nice rooms, huh?' said his father. 'I see you've managed to put your bag down. Any chance of unpacking?'

'What?' mumbled Alex.

His father walked across and joined him at the window.

'It's a good view, isn't it?' Then, noticing his son's troubled face he asked, 'Are you OK?'

Alex opened his mouth to speak, but then nodded his head. What could he say? His dad would think he was scared because he was in his own room. Maybe he was. Maybe he was just being childish, he thought – frightening himself over nothing.

'Yeah,' said Alex with a weak smile. 'I just wondered if we were going to get something to eat?'

'Of course,' said his father. 'How hungry are you?'

'Starving,' said Alex.

'Hah!' said his father. 'You're always starving. How do pancakes sound? It's kind of a speciality here.'

'Great,' said Alex.

'Unpack your stuff and then we'll head straight out.'

Alex was already feeling better. Whatever it was that had jangled his nerves a few moments ago seemed to have utterly vanished. His father went back to his room and Alex unpacked his case.

Alex and his father headed for the pancake house the receptionist had recommended, walking along the canal and then over a humpback bridge lined with bicycles chained to the railings. A tourist boat puttered by beneath them and Alex could hear the sonorous voice of the guide pointing out buildings they passed.

Clouds still darkened the sky above the serrated roofline of the canal-side buildings but the drizzle that had been falling when they left the hotel was now dying away. The street had seemed almost sleepy from his hotel room, but down at street level it was anything but. The break in rain showers had brought the area back to life.

Cars and delivery vehicles now rumbled along the canal-side road, and cyclists sped this way and that. Only tourists walked, Alex noticed, and even then some of those wobbled by on hired bikes. There were bikes everywhere.

They were ridden by all kinds of people: stylish older women in expensive-looking clothes, young women in short skirts with long hair trailing behind them, men in suits, chatting on their mobile phones, their ties flapping over their shoulders.

Once over the bridge Alex and his father walked up the street facing them, past a row of shops and a cluster of tourists gathered round a map. Alex's father put down the umbrella he had borrowed from the hotel as the rain stopped entirely and grinned at his son.

'Great, isn't it?' he said. 'I love this city.'

Alex nodded as he stepped out of the path of a cyclist. It was great.

'Look, this is it!'

Next to a café was the pancake house they were looking for, metal chairs and tables on the pavement under a blue-and-white striped awning. A group of Americans were leaving, kissing and embracing before they went their separate ways.

Alex and his father sat outside as the rain had stopped. The remains of the last shower dripped from the awning. It was humid and the clouds threatened thunder at any moment, but Alex was glad to be outside. It was nice to sit and watch the world go by.

It was a narrow, busy little street and although few cars passed by there was a constant stream of motorbikes, scooters and bicycles, pinging their bells loudly as they rode past.

'What do you fancy, Alex?' asked his father.

'I don't know,' he said, scanning the long list of

possibilities with a look of bafflement on his face. The menu was in English, but the choice was dizzying.

'Have a bacon one,' said his father, pointing it out. 'You'll like that.'

'OK,' said Alex, relieved to have the decision taken from him.

'I'm going to have a coffee,' said his father. 'How about you? Do you want a fruit juice or a fizzy water or something?'

'No – I'll have a coffee as well.'

'Really?' said his father. 'Since when did you drink coffee?'

'Since ages ago,' said Alex. It was actually only a few months since he had discovered a taste for it.

The waitress came over and though she greeted them in English, Alex's father replied in Dutch. Alex smiled at his father when she had gone. It was funny hearing him speak Dutch.

'It's a weird language,' said Alex, when the waitress had gone. 'It sounds like you're swearing all the time.'

His father laughed. 'I wonder what we sound like to them?' he said.

The pancakes were huge – like pizzas, overlapping the plates they were on. Strips of bacon were laid across them in rows.

'They look good,' said his father. He reached out and grabbed a small plastic bottle and began to squeeze the contents over his pancakes.

'What's that?' asked Alex, curling his lip.

'Syrup,' said his father. 'Try some.'

'Syrup?' said Alex. 'On bacon?'

'Just try it,' said his father. 'They do the same in the US. When you come to New York –'

'New York?' said Alex. 'We're going to New York? Cool! When are we –'

'Whoa there,' said his father. 'I didn't say we'd be going next week.'

'But sometime?' said Alex.

Alex's father grinned.

'Absolutely.'

'Yes!' said Alex punching the air.

Daniel Forbes in his English class had never shut up about his trip to New York the previous autumn – or 'fall' as he had insisted on calling it ever since.

When they had finished their pancakes, his father waved at the waitress and mouthed something in Dutch. She nodded and went away to fetch the bill.

'I'll take you back to the hotel,' said his father. 'Saskia will be picking me up soon.'

'What about me?'

'Sorry, Alex,' said his father. 'You know that I have

to work while I'm here. They are paying for the trip after all.'

'Yeah, I know,' said Alex. 'But it's going to be really boring if all I do is hang out at the hotel every day.'

'It won't be every day, Alex,' said his father.

'Yeah, but it's going to be today, isn't it?'

'Well,' said his father, 'we may have solved that problem. Angelien has agreed to show you round.'

'What?' said Alex. 'Dad!'

'Come on, Alex,' said his father. 'It's really nice of Saskia to suggest it and good of Angelien to volunteer her time.'

'I don't even *know* her!' said Alex, staring down at the table.

'Well now's your chance.' His father stood up and handed some euro notes to the waitress.

Alex opened his mouth to protest but his father raised his hands.

'I don't want to hear it, Alex,' he said, more firmly now. 'I agreed with your headmaster that you could take time off school. We both know why. His only stipulation was that you produce a written piece about your visit. Angelien will be a very good guide, I'm sure.'

Alex had wondered how long it would be before his father mentioned the business at school. He scowled but made no reply. There was no point in picking at that scab, he knew.

21

3

Alex stared sullenly out of the lobby window. The recent showers had splashed the glass with a million droplets of water and the view through them was blurred and confused, like seeing through a fly's eyes.

'Is everything OK?' said Saskia, casting a quick glance towards Alex.

'Everything is perfect,' said his father.

Saskia raised her eyebrows.

His father sighed. 'He's not a happy bunny,' he said. 'He's cross with me because I can't spend the afternoon with him.'

Saskia nodded and looked sympathetic.

'We have to borrow your father for a while, I'm afraid. But Angelien will look after you,' said Saskia, 'won't you, my darling?'

'Of course,' said Angelien.

Alex frowned doubtfully and Angelien laughed.

'OK then,' said Alex's father. 'I'll see you later. Bye, Alex.'

Alex grunted a reply that could have been almost anything. His father knew better than to wait for more and simply turned and left with Saskia at his side.

Alex watched them walk away, arm in arm, along the canal. He heard Saskia's laughter twitter in the clear morning air like birdsong.

Their happiness bothered him and he felt bad that it did. His mother had gone off with someone else after all. Why shouldn't his father be happy?

'Well,' said Angelien, with a crooked grin. 'My mother has given me a wallet full of euros so why don't we go and spend it? What would you like to do?'

Alex shrugged. He stared off towards the diminishing figures of his father and Saskia.

'I don't know.'

'What do you say we just walk around for a while?' said Angelien. 'It seems a shame to spend the afternoon in museums as it's not raining. When I'm somewhere new, I like to walk around and get a feeling for a place.'

'OK,' said Alex.

'What do you know about Amsterdam?'

Alex shrugged again and looked sheepish. His father had given him a guidebook to read but he had only flicked through it, looking at the photographs.

'Not a lot,' he said.

Angelien laughed. 'OK. I will tell you a few things. Where to start? Well, Amsterdam was founded in the thirteenth century. It was just a little village at first, but grew and grew. It has always been a trading place, sending ships all over the world . . .'

Alex wasn't really listening to what Angelien was saying but was concentrating instead on her lips. They had a strange way of pouting intermittently as she spoke, and he watched, fascinated. She wasn't just pretty like a couple of the girls were at his school. She was better than pretty.

'. . . is called the Golden Age. That was the greatest time for Amsterdam. The houses like the one you are staying in are from that time.

'You see the tops of the houses?' she said, pointing to the buildings along the canal. Alex looked, the spell of Angelien's lips broken for the moment. 'Do you see that door with the pole sticking out above it?'

'I thought it was a window,' said Alex.

'No,' said Angelien. 'It's a door into an attic warehouse. Many of them still have the winching gear on them for hauling the stuff up to the top of the house.'

'So they were warehouses?'

'They were homes as well as warehouses,' said Angelien.

Looking down the length of the canal, Alex saw for the first time how many of these houses there were. Angelien seemed to read his mind.

'Amsterdam was built for business. It was one big shop. It has always been about making money. Spending it too, of course . . .' she said.

'They must have been stinking rich,' said Alex.

Angelien laughed.

'Stinking rich?' she said. 'I like that: stinking rich! Ha! They were indeed, Alex.'

A small white boat passed under the bridge and someone called Angelien's name. There were two well-dressed men and two women aboard. She waved back.

'Friends of my mother,' said Angelien. 'They are "stinking rich".'

Alex laughed.

'Come on,' she said. 'Let's walk. Before it starts raining again.'

Angelien set off with Alex at her side, turning left and right down narrow alleyways and wide, busy streets. She pointed out buildings and tiny details that Alex would never have noticed without her.

'Amsterdam's really pretty,' said Alex as they

walked down a picturesque canal, lined with small trees and shops. 'My dad just goes on about the war, so I suppose I never really thought much about how it looked now.'

Angelien nodded.

'This is a tough place,' she said. 'We've been through a lot.'

Angelien looked away and her smile disappeared.

'There were eighty thousand Jews living here before the Nazis came and only five thousand when the war ended.'

'We did about Anne Frank at school,' said Alex. 'And Dad has told me loads of stuff about World War Two. I don't remember all of it. It must have been horrible though. To be occupied I mean.'

Angelien nodded and her lips quivered a little before she spoke.

'My grandmother told me such terrible things about that time... About the war and the time after.'

Alex saw the sadness on Angelien's face but could think of nothing to say. After a moment, she smiled and clapped her hands together, snapping out of the grip of those memories.

'Enough of sadness,' she said. 'There's more to Amsterdam than sad memories, huh?'

They walked on. Alex was surprised at how

relaxed he was already feeling in Angelien's company.

'This is the Looier,' said Angelien as they rounded a corner near a wide canal. 'It's an antiques market – but indoors. Lots of it is very expensive but it is interesting. Do you want to go in?'

Alex shrugged and nodded at the same time. There was a man nearby who was sitting outside his workshop polishing a table leg that lay across his lap. Angelien walked inside and Alex smiled at him, but he just looked away, and carried on with his work.

Inside there were rows of glass cabinets with glass shelves, on which were collections of objects. The cabinets were themed: one had metal toys, another dour Victorian photographs in dusty old frames. There was a cabinet full of military medals and badges and then another nearby filled with old wooden and metal crucifixes. Alex guessed this must be where the hotel manager's wife had come to buy things for the hotel.

Every now and then a dealer had a larger area to themselves, almost like a small shop within the market. There was a man selling old books. He was sitting in a leather armchair reading, and only looked up briefly to establish that neither Angelien nor Alex seemed likely customers.

Nearby a woman was selling old ceramic tiles. Angelien stopped and pointed them out to Alex. Each one had a drawing on it, usually in blue line. Alex picked one up that had a drawing of a man aiming a shotgun at a bird flying overhead. When Alex saw the price sticker, he turned to Angelien in amazement.

'That much for an old tile?' he gasped.

'These are very old, Alex,' she said. 'There are lots of fakes around but these are the real thing.'

The owner nodded at Angelien's remark and then gave Alex a rather less friendly glare over her half-moon glasses. Alex put the tile back, embarrassed, and pretended to be interested in another, this time with a young girl on it. The tile was cracked across from one corner to the other and a chip had fallen out just where the girl's face ought to be. There was something troubling about the faceless image.

Alex turned to follow Angelien, who was already heading for a doorway through to a room which looked more like a school jumble sale.

'This is a room where people can just book a table and set themselves up to sell whatever they have. A lot of it is junk, of course.' She grinned. 'But still I can't resist hunting about. Shall we have a look and see if we can't find treasure?'

Angelien had started rooting around in a box filled with doorknobs, when a raucous dance track started up that Alex did not initially realise was Angelien's ringtone. It was very loud by the time she had dug her phone out and answered the call. An old man nearby scowled at her.

'Hallo? Dirk!'

Angelien turned her back on Alex and walked away a few steps as she talked, walking to an open doorway and out into the street. She turned and looked at him through the window before going back to her conversation.

Alex walked on to another stall and looked at some battered old metal toy cars. He picked up a chipped and worn old truck, remembering the fun he used to have with a similar toy when he was a small boy. But that memory only led to thoughts of his mother.

He put the truck down and moved on again. It was then that he saw it, lying in an old tea crate on top of a pile of odds and ends, partially obscured by an old scarf.

It was a mask.

Not the kind worn by superheroes and highwaymen that covers just your eyes; this mask was a full face and quite an old one, judging by the cracked and worn white surface. Its empty eyes seemed to stare up at him and he leaned over to pick it up.

It was lighter than he had expected and, turning it over to look at the inside, he found that it was made of wood. It was also surprisingly cold to the touch. He turned it back over to look at the oval face.

It seemed to be a mask of an old woman. A small nose rose up from the curved oval and a mouth opened beneath that, small and smiling, a thin black crescent lying on its back, the upturned points ending in three carved creases.

The eyes were almost the same shape as the mouth, though the other way round so that they pointed downwards, and with softer ends closest to the nose. Above the eyes there were no eyebrows, just a succession of shallow wrinkles. There were more wrinkles below the eyes. The stallholder – a young woman in a heavy sweater and a woollen hat, long red hair parted on either side of her round face – started talking to him in Dutch and then, realising he didn't understand, switched to English.

'It's interesting, no?' she said. 'Maybe Japanese. You like it?'

Alex shook his head and put the mask down. But he had only walked on a few paces when something made him stop and turn round. The mask looked back at him from the stall where he had set it down.

Alex was held by the mask's inscrutable gaze. The vacant eyes seemed to have him in a hypnotic grip and he reached out to pick it up again.

'How much is it?'

Alex actually disliked the mask quite strongly. But he also knew that for some reason he wanted it.

'For you – twenty euros,' she said, pushing her hair away from her face, leaving a long strand stuck to her lipstick. It slashed across her face like a long red scar.

Alex's father had only given him twenty euros to spend for the whole of that day. It was a lot of money, but even so, he knew he had to have it.

'OK,' said Alex.

Alex handed the mask to the stallholder. He reached inside his jacket and took out his wallet, then counted out the notes and handed them over. The woman counted the money and lifted her sweater to put it in a zip-up purse on her belt.

'I'll put some paper around it,' she said. 'Would you like a bag?'

'Yes please,' said Alex, now wondering whether he should have haggled about the price. Angelien walked over just as Alex was taking the bag from the stallholder.

'Hey, I wondered where you were for a minute,' said Angelien. 'What have you bought?'

'A mask,' said Alex. 'Do you want to see?'

'Sure,' she said. 'But how about getting something to eat?'

Alex nodded.

'Who was that on the phone?' he asked. 'Your boyfriend?'

Angelien smiled and pursed her lips.

'None of your business,' she said.

Angelien led the way and after a few minutes they arrived at another pancake house. It was much bigger than the one he had been to with his father at lunchtime. This one was like a fast food place, with rows of plastic-covered tables and vases of plastic tulips.

The waiters all said hello when she came in and a woman came round from behind the counter and kissed her on both cheeks.

'I used to work here,' said Angelien, when they had sat down at a table by the window. 'I was a waitress for months when I was starting college. It's hard work though – my feet were so sore at the end of the evening . . . What is that phrase you English say when your feet hurt?'

Alex shrugged. 'I don't know.'

'Sure you do,' Angelien said, frowning as she tried to remember. 'I hate it when I can't remember.'

A waiter came over and Angelien ordered a bacon pancake. Alex did the same.

Alex smiled. He still didn't really know what to say to Angelien and was happier looking out of the window than into her face. He knew a few girls at school but he had never had a real girlfriend or been on a date. He had never even been alone with a girl like this in a café. Since the trouble with Molly, none of the girls at school would speak to him. They just ignored him completely or giggled and walked away.

Alex looked out of the window, watching cyclists sail through the junction, seemingly fearless of cars and motorbikes. A garbage truck beeped as it reversed over the wheel of a bicycle chained to a tree. The driver craned round to look at what he'd hit and then drove off, leaving the bicycle wheel bent and useless.

'Killing me!' shouted Angelien suddenly, slapping her palm down on the table and making Alex jump.

'What?' said Alex.

'"My feet are killing me",' she said with a grin. 'That is what you say. I love that saying.'

Angelien chuckled to herself.

The waiter brought their order. Angelien started eating her pancake, rolling her eyes and sighing. 'The pancakes are so good here.'

Alex poured syrup in a thin spiral over his own.

'So how about you? Do you have a girlfriend?'

Alex shrugged and looked at the table.

'Nah,' he said.

'How come?' said Angelien leaning forward and peering up into Alex's lowered face. 'A good-looking boy like you?'

'I just haven't, OK?' said Alex, frowning.

Angelien laughed.

'OK, OK,' she said. 'So what did you buy?' said Angelien, sitting back in her chair and waving to the waiter.

'A mask,' said Alex.

The waiter came over and stood next to the table.

'*Een koffie en* . . . Alex, what would you like to drink?'

'Can I have tea?' said Alex.

'*Een thee, alsjeblieft.*'

The waiter walked away to fetch their drinks.

Alex unwrapped the tissue paper and passed the mask across the table. Angelien took it carefully, and laid the mask on top of the tissue paper.

'The woman said it might be Japanese,' he said.

Angelien studied the mask intently for a few moments and then looked back at Alex.

'Is something the matter?' he asked.

Angelien put her hands to the side of her face and frowned, obviously deep in thought.

'But . . . But this is so strange . . .'

'What is?' said Alex.

'Well –'

'Angelien!' a voice called out from behind them.

'Dirk!' said Angelien, turning round and getting up. A man was walking over to them. He was tall and slim, with long tangled hair that was heading towards dreadlocks. He had a long face with stubble growing over his cleft chin. Angelien kissed him and they hugged. He looked over Angelien's shoulder and smiled a crooked smile at Alex.

'What a surprise,' said Angelien.

Alex knew that she was speaking in English for his benefit, and he wasn't fooled. She had arranged to meet this man here, Alex was sure. He wrapped the mask up again and put it back in the bag.

'Sit down,' said Angelien. 'We were just about to pay. Dirk – this is Alex, from England.'

'Alex,' said Dirk with a nod.

He sat down, slouching back and stretching his long legs out. A long key chain dangled from a clip on a belt loop on his hip, and rattled against the chair as he moved forward.

'I'm taking Alex on a tour of Amsterdam,' said Angelien. 'Why don't you come along? Alex won't mind, will you, Alex?'

Alex shrugged and finished his tea.

'Sure,' said Dirk with a wide grin. 'Perhaps I'll learn something, huh?'

Angelien paid the bill and they left the pancake house. Dirk put his arm around Angelien's waist and pulled her towards him. She stumbled a little, laughing. Alex sighed.

For a while, Angelien continued to point things out to Alex and tell him about them, but more and more, Dirk would interrupt in Dutch and the two of them would start a conversation that Alex could not understand.

Alex found himself trailing along behind them. As they approached yet another bridge over yet another canal, Alex came to a halt and let them walk on. A busker started singing across the street. A black-and-white cat brushed up against his legs.

Alex wondered how long it would take them to notice he was no longer there, but they were already over the bridge and had not realised. Alex scowled and turned back the way they had come. The cat scurried away.

To find his own way back, all he had to do was follow the main road they had just come from until he reached the big square near the hotel. He knew his way from there.

But after walking steadily for ten minutes Alex recognised nothing and realised that he must have turned the wrong way. Or maybe this was not the main road he thought it was. He didn't even know which direction he was walking in.

He stood on the side of a small canal as the rain began to fall again. A girl ran by in a red hooded coat and her reflection dripped into the water like blood.

Alex cursed and stared at the sky, raindrops spitting in his face. Suddenly all of Amsterdam looked exactly the same. He unzipped his jacket and took out his mobile phone.

4

Alex's father, Saskia and Angelien were standing outside the hotel. Alex couldn't hear what they were saying but he could see that his father was angry, even though he was barely saying a word.

Saskia, on the other hand, was saying enough for the two of them. She was red in the face and wagging her finger furiously at Angelien who was looking uncomfortable.

After a few minutes Angelien came into the hotel and walked over. She sat down opposite him. She picked up a sachet of sugar from the bowl on the table, and tapped it a few times before tossing it down.

'Why did you just walk off like that?' she said. 'I looked everywhere for you.'

Alex shrugged.

'I was worried about you,' she said.

'Yeah?' muttered Alex.

'I'm really sorry about what happened,' said Angelien. 'All right?'

'No offence,' said Alex, 'but I didn't even want to go round Amsterdam with you. I wanted to go with my dad.'

Angelien glanced at her mother who was still talking to Alex's father outside.

'Look,' she said, dropping her voice. 'I thought it was a dumb idea too, if you really want to know.'

'Then why did you agree to do it?' said Alex.

Angelien opened her mouth as if to say something, but thought better of it and took a deep breath instead.

'Because I care about my mother and I would like her to be happy,' she said with a sigh.

Angelien reached out and touched his hand.

'I promise there will be no more Dirk,' she said, squeezing his fingers. 'He wouldn't even help me to look for you. Look, Alex, I got into big trouble. Your father thinks I am not a responsible person and my mother – my mother says she is going to kill me. I wish that were true – at least it would be quick. She is going to go on and on at me for weeks. Please don't give me a hard time too. Please. We're friends, huh?'

Alex took a deep breath. Despite the whole business with Dirk, Alex liked Angelien.

He knew he could not stay cross with her. He

hadn't had much fun of late, and Angelien was fun to be with. He smiled.

'OK,' he said.

'In any case, we need to talk about that mask you bought,' said Angelien with a smile.

'I know,' said Alex. 'My dad went mental when I told him I'd paid twenty euros for it.'

Angelien rolled her eyes.

'Bah!' she said. 'Another thing that was my fault apparently. But it doesn't matter. Anyway, that's not what I meant. The mask is –' Angelien saw Saskia walking back and grabbed Alex's hand. 'Please, Alex – be nice to me. Pleeeeease.'

'So,' said Saskia, walking towards them. 'Has my daughter apologised?'

'Yes,' said Alex. 'It's OK. Everything's cool.'

'Everything is most certainly not "cool",' said Saskia with a frown. 'It is not "cool" at all.'

'Mother!' said Angelien. 'Come on. I've said sorry and Alex has accepted. What more do you want me to do? I can't do anything about what happened.'

'It was my fault as well,' said Alex. 'For walking off. I shouldn't have done it and I've caused a fuss and everything. I'm really sorry.'

'You would not have walked off if she hadn't been with that no-good –'

'OK, OK,' said Angelien, burying her face in her

hands. Angelien mumbled some words in Dutch without taking her hands away.

Saskia stood stiffly for a few moments and then turned to Alex.

'Jeremy needs to come into the office again tomorrow,' she said, in a softer tone of voice.

'Again?' said Alex. 'He said he would have some time off tomorrow.'

'I'm afraid not,' said Saskia. 'If today had not been so disrupted . . .'

Saskia glared at Angelien, who scowled and looked out of the window. Alex's father eventually walked over.

'Look. What's done is done,' he said. 'Angelien has apologised and has agreed to spend tomorrow with you. But only if you agree. If you aren't happy about it, we will have to think of something else.'

Angelien looked at Alex with big, pleading eyes.

'It's fine,' he said. 'Really.'

'Good,' said Saskia. 'Let's hope we can all start over. Beginning with tonight. We will pick you up for dinner at seven o'clock.'

5

Alex stood under the shower, lost to the white-noise hiss and the pin-sharp drumming of the water on his head and neck. Alex's father had insisted that he had a shower before they went out, and he'd thought it best not to argue. He stepped out, a little light-headed, drying himself on a huge white towel.

Standing in front of the bathroom mirror, he had the same uncanny feeling he'd had earlier in the day: that there was someone watching him; as if the mirror was one of those two-way devices he had seen in TV programmes and cop movies where you could look at someone but they could not see you – they only saw their own reflection. A drip from his wet hair trickled down his back and made him shiver.

Alex put on the hotel bathrobe and went back into the bedroom, closing the door on the bathroom and the mirror, and telling himself he was being stupid.

He had put the mask, still in its bag, on the top of a chest of drawers near the connecting door to his father's room. A sombre-looking carriage clock sat on top of this chest and Alex wondered if that too was the result of one of those trips to the antiques market.

Its tick was more of a gasp or a quiet cough, as though someone was repeatedly trying to clear their throat.

He remembered how the manager had said that his wife had felt the objects she bought spoke to her. Alex thought he understood this now. The mask had not spoken actual words, but the effect was the same. It was as though the mask had reeled him in like a fish on a line.

Alex picked the mask up and inspected it. Again he was surprised at how cold it was to the touch. Though it was made of wood, it was chilled like a piece of marble.

He ran his fingers over the smooth nose and mouth and around the curved teardrop-like eye sockets. It had been white once, and skull-smooth, but age had yellowed it and crazed the varnished surface so that it looked like cracked eggshell.

There was something about its inscrutable, frozen smile that Alex found horribly disconcerting. His head still felt hot from the shower and the dizziness returned as he squinted at the mask. It now seemed utterly repugnant to him. Why had he found it so hard to resist it at the antiques market?

He opened a drawer in the chest and slid the mask inside, then closed it again a little more forcefully than he had intended.

Five minutes later he was following his father into the lift and down to where Saskia and Angelien were already waiting for them in their usual spot in the hotel lobby.

'We haven't kept you waiting, I hope,' said Alex's father.

'No, no,' said Saskia, standing up to kiss him. 'We were early.'

'Mum's always early,' said Angelien, moving her bag so that Alex could sit down. 'She always panics about being late.'

'There's nothing wrong with wanting to be on time,' said Saskia. 'You're young and pretty. You can be as late as you like and no one minds.

'So – we are going to take you to a little restaurant we know. We can walk – it's not too far. Shall we go?'

They all got to their feet and headed for the door. It was no longer raining, but the street was still wet and Alex shivered at the dampness in the air as they stepped outside.

They left the hotel behind them and walked along the canal. A group of tourists walked past in the opposite direction. The wet cobbles were almost as reflective as the black waters of the canal and a distorted mirror image of the group trailed in their wake as they walked away.

Saskia had set off ahead. Alex's father caught up with her and they linked arms. As they crossed the bridge, Alex couldn't resist looking back towards his room. He would never have admitted it, even to himself, but he half expected to see something – a silhouette on the curtains, a face at the window.

Alex felt foolish for feeling uneasy and yet the uneasiness remained. He had never experienced anything like this. He had no idea what he was afraid of or why.

There was no face at the window, no sinister silhouette. The light was off, just as he had left it. Angelien saw him looking back and followed his gaze.

'Forgotten something?' she asked.

'No . . .' said Alex, starting at her voice. 'I thought I saw something.'

Angelien smiled, scanning his face.

'Anything in particular?'

Alex shrugged. He looked at the hotel again. It was just a trick of light, he was sure, probably caused by the position of the street lights and the fact that other rooms had their lights on, but the window of his room seemed darker somehow. The glass was so black it could have been blocked up and painted.

'No . . . not really.'

Angelien gave him a quizzical look but didn't say anything more.

'Angelien is studying the houses along this canal,' said Saskia, her voice bright and cheerful.

'Really?' said Alex's father, turning to look at Angelien. 'How come?'

'My doctorate is on family life in seventeenth-century Amsterdam,' said Angelien. 'I am using this canal as the basis for the study.'

Alex turned away from the hotel. He seemed to feel its chill on his back like ice and shivered slightly as he walked.

'Are you studying our house?' said Alex. 'I mean the house that's been turned into our hotel?'

Angelien nodded. 'I was just looking at some papers about it the other day, in fact,' she said.

They were walking down a busy street now and the crowds and the conversation seemed to have a magical effect. Alex felt entirely normal once more. As strange as the sensation of dread had been, the immediacy of its lifting was, if anything, even stranger.

'Are you interested in history, Alex?' said Saskia.

'I suppose so,' he replied. 'A bit. I like the Romans.'

'He's *obsessed* by the Romans,' said his father.

'No I'm not,' said Alex, blushing a little. 'I just think they're cool, that's all.'

'And so they are,' said Angelien and, to Alex's surprise, she linked her arm with his. The fur of her hood brushed his face as she leaned in and whispered, 'Romans are very cool.'

Alex felt his heart race at her touch. He had never walked arm in arm with anyone. That was something people did in the movies. It felt nice though. Saskia and his father had moved on. A distant tram sounded its horn.

'What did you mean about the mask earlier?' said Alex. 'What did you want to tell me?'

Angelien cast a quick glance towards her mother and put her fingers to her lips.

'Tomorrow,' she said. 'It's too weird to talk about now. Too crazy . . .'

She nodded her head towards their parents and headed after them with Alex in tow, wondering what she meant by 'Too crazy'.

'Here we are!' announced Saskia. Alex's father turned and raised his eyebrow slightly when he saw Angelien and Alex arm in arm.

They were outside a brightly lit restaurant with a sign that had tropical leaves painted on it in gold. A blast of warm air full of strange aromas hit Alex's face as he walked in. A waitress, small and dark skinned, dressed in black, smiled and came across to show them to a table.

The contrast between the dark buildings outside and the restaurant interior was startling. It was warm and lit by fairy lights and small candles on the tables. There were potted plants everywhere. It felt as though they had been transported to the tropics.

The conversation was a little strained at first, as everyone tried to avoid all mention of what had happened that afternoon.

Saskia ordered a host of small dishes from the menu and when the food arrived Alex liked most of what he tried, though he found it hard to predict what flavour anything was going to have. Many of the flavours were ones he had never experienced before.

Alex hadn't realised how tired he had become after the flight and the meal helped to revive him. He wondered if tiredness was the source of his earlier jitters. It seemed a comforting explanation.

'You seem to like the food, Alex,' said Saskia with a wide smile.

'Yeah,' said Alex. 'It's delicious. Weird though.'

Saskia laughed. Alex smiled back. She had a nice laugh.

'So your teachers don't mind you not being at school?' asked Saskia, as the waitress poured her another glass of wine. 'They don't mind you missing lessons while you're here?'

Alex and his father exchanged a quick glance and Alex could see from the panic in his face that he thought Alex was going to tell them about the business with Molly Ryman, but why would he do that?

'The head teacher gave him a special leave of absence,' said his father, 'provided that he writes an essay about his visit.'

Saskia nodded and smiled.

'What are you going to write about?' asked Saskia.

Alex shifted in his chair. He had given this no thought whatsoever.

'Mother!' said Angelien. 'How can he know what he's going to write about? He's only been here a day.'

'I just thought –' began Saskia.

'So, you've been studying the townhouses on our hotel's stretch of the canal,' said Alex's father, turning to Angelien. 'Have you learned anything about our hotel?'

Alex noticed the look on Saskia's face as she was interrupted. He'd seen that look on his mother's face many times. His father just didn't seem to listen sometimes.

'A little, yes,' said Angelien. 'A lot actually. I may be using it as the centre of my study.'

'Really?' said Saskia. 'You never told me that.'

'You never asked,' said Angelien with a shrug.

'It was a merchant's house in the 1650s,' continued Angelien. 'All the houses along there were merchant's houses. They are very typical actually.'

'Do you know who owned that particular one?' asked Alex's father. 'The hotel?'

'It was a man called Johannes Van Kampen. He was rich, staunchly Protestant. He made his money trading with the Dutch East India Company – with Japan mainly.'

Alex's father nodded and looked at Alex.

'It's amazing to think that old Van Kampen and his family were wandering around in our bedrooms three hundred and fifty years ago, isn't it?'

'Yeah,' said Alex.

And it was amazing, he thought. The house had stood there for centuries and who knew how many people had lived and died in it. Somehow it made the hotel seem different. That dimly lit street and those dark houses with their big blank windows. There were new buildings among the old in that part of Amsterdam, but somehow the old buildings won through, despite the cars and the trams. The past seemed closer there.

'It's good that you made up with Angelien,' said Alex's father as he stood in the doorway that connected their two rooms.

'Yeah,' said Alex matter-of-factly.

'You'll be OK with her again tomorrow?' said his father with a raised eyebrow.

'It's fine,' said Alex with a yawn. 'I don't mind.'

'Less drama this time.'

Alex nodded.

'Well OK then. Goodnight, champ.'

'Night, Dad,' said Alex.

Alex's father switched off the main light and went through to his room, closing the door behind him. Alex switched off the bedside light, yawned and pulled the duvet up around him, sinking into the pillows, and almost immediately slid into a deep sleep, filled with tangled dreams, where Amsterdam and England were one impossible place filled with a confusion of faces old and new.

But he hadn't been asleep long when he was dragged back from these dreaming depths and into a wary consciousness. He had the strongest sensation that something was in the room with him. He sat up, peering suspiciously into the gloom around him. There was nothing there, he was sure. That is, he was sure and yet not sure.

He turned on the bedside light. Alex was startled to see that the mask he had bought was now on top of the chest of drawers. He hadn't noticed it there before he got into bed. He looked around the room for any other sign of disturbance but everything was just as he had left it: everything apart from the mask.

Someone must have been in his room. Maybe the maid had been going through his stuff? But why? And in any case the maids worked in the morning, not the evening.

Alex heard his father walking round the room next door. Had his father come in and looked through the drawers?

Alex looked towards the connecting door, scowling. What was his father doing going through his stuff? He looked down at the mask, opened the drawer and slid it inside once again.

Alex got back into bed and turned out the light. He shivered, pulling the duvet tight about his face and body so that he was wrapped up like a mummy. Still he felt cold, as though the temperature had dropped ten degrees. He wondered if the air conditioning was to blame but didn't want to get out of bed to check.

Alex closed his eyes. He was tired, so very tired. If he could just distract himself from whatever was unnerving him for long enough, he knew that he would fall asleep.

And Angelien's face appeared in his mind's eye, like sunshine in a dark well. There was something about her that warmed him, relaxed him. He relived their walk together, a walk that now seemed bathed in sunshine rather than threatened by rain. In no time at all he was drifting away with her down the canal in a white boat and off into a peaceful sleep.

6

A barge sounded its horn on the canal outside and Alex woke suddenly, fully alert, with a disturbing sensation that something had woken him.

A milky morning light was seeping lazily through the floral curtains and making the room glow.

The barge sounded its horn again and Alex realised that this must be what had woken him.

He pushed the duvet away and got out of bed. He opened a drawer in the chest and there was the mask staring back at him with its dark, empty eyes. He took out a pair of socks and hurriedly closed the drawer, but seeing the mask reminded him of his suspicion that his father had been going through his things.

'Dad,' he said, when his silence over breakfast had been ignored. 'Have you been in my room?'

'Course I have,' he said, slurping his coffee. 'What do you mean?'

'When I was asleep. Have you been going through my stuff?'

'Going through your stuff?' repeated his dad, putting down the newspaper he was reading. 'You haven't got much stuff to go through, have you?'

'I'm serious, Dad,' said Alex, finding his father's joking annoying. 'There's no point in us having our own rooms if you –'

His father reached out and put his hand on Alex's sleeve.

'I promise you,' he said. 'I have not been going through your things. OK?'

Alex scanned his father's face for any sign that this was not the complete truth, and found none. His father was a terrible liar anyway. But if he hadn't been in his room, then who had?

After breakfast they found Saskia and Angelien once more waiting for them in the lobby downstairs. As soon as Saskia and Alex's father had gone, Angelien grabbed Alex by the arm.

'Before we go, can I take another look at the mask, Alex?' she said.

'I . . . suppose so,' said Alex, unsure of whether he ought to be agreeing to this. He could see his father and Saskia through the hotel window, crossing the canal. 'It's in my room.'

'OK,' said Angelien, patting him on the back. 'Let's go.'

After a moment's hesitation, Alex went back to reception and asked for his key and then took Angelien to the lifts, ignoring the arched eyebrows of the receptionist. While they were in the lift, Angelien noticed Alex's key and the brooch attached to it.

'The manager's wife found loads· of different things to use as key rings,' said Alex.

'It's old,' said Angelien. 'It's a bit battered about but it was probably a pretty brooch once.'

Alex unlocked the door and showed Angelien in. She whistled appreciatively as they stepped inside.

'Hey – nice room,' she said, walking across to the window. 'And nice view too.'

As Alex let Angelien into his room, he was suddenly aware of how untidy it was and tried hurriedly to kick his clothes into a neat pile on the floor.

'Don't bother,' said Angelien, turning away from the window. 'You should see my room. I am the messiest person alive, believe me.'

Angelien sat down on the bed and tested the springs. Then she flopped backwards, looking up at the ceiling. Her jacket fell open to reveal a white T-shirt with a red-and-blue target design across the chest. A sliver of pale flesh showed between the

T-shirt and her faded blue jeans. Alex stood staring at her until she sat up, grinning at him.

'Well?' she said.

'W . . . What?' said Alex.

'The mask? Remember?'

'Yeah . . . right,' mumbled Alex, turning and banging his arm against the chest of drawers and wincing.

Alex opened the drawer, picked up the mask and handed it to her. She held it in her left hand, running the fingers of her right hand lightly over its cracked surface. She took a deep breath and let it out slowly with a puzzled look on her face.

'What is it?' said Alex.

'It will sound crazy enough,' said Angelien, 'so I think the best way is for me to show you.'

'Show me what?'

'Come on,' she said. 'Let's go now. I'm probably wrong anyway.'

'Wrong about what?' said Alex.

'There is something I want to show you,' she said.

Alex had no idea what Angelien was talking about but was curious enough to want to find out. He locked up the room and they left the hotel.

Angelien set off across a nearby bridge and down a narrow alleyway that opened up on to a wide street criss-crossed with tramlines.

'If we're quick, we can catch that one,' said Angelien as a tram rounded the corner, its wheels whistling and grating on the rails.

Alex ran to keep up with Angelien and they reached the tram stop just as the doors opened and a small queue of people began to step aboard. Angelien paid the driver.

They sat down, the doors shut and the tram moved away with a hum and a faint clanking. It stopped at a set of lights before setting off up a long straight and very wide avenue.

'So where are we going?' asked Alex.

'To the Rijksmuseum,' she answered.

'The what?' said Alex.

'Rijksmuseum,' said Angelien, over the whining of a tram as it rounded a bend.

'And there's something there to do with my mask?' he asked. 'Is that it?'

'Wait and see,' said Angelien.

They both looked out of the window as the tram continued on its way crossing bridge after bridge, canal after canal, until Angelien signalled it was time to get off.

They walked along the Singel canal for a while. The sky was filthy grey and a murky twilight had descended.

Another glass-roofed tour boat went by, filled

with passengers. Alex could hear the voice of the guide on board but couldn't recognise the language. It started to spit with rain as they reached a large, rather grim-looking building partially obscured by construction hoardings. A steady stream of people were crossing the road ahead of them.

'So is this the place?' said Alex.

'The Rijksmuseum,' said Angelien.

'It looks like a building site,' said Alex. 'Is it open?'

'Yes,' she said. 'Well – not all of it. It is an art museum – like your National Gallery in London. It is very well known. It has paintings by Vermeer, Frans Hals and Rembrandt and lots of other famous painters. You've never heard of it?'

Alex shook his head. They crossed the road and followed the painted arrows that led round the side of the building.

'Do you like paintings?' Angelien asked Alex, as she handed her bag to the security guard.

'Yeah,' said Alex. 'Some paintings.'

Alex passed his bag over as well and they waited for them to emerge from the scanner. Then they checked them into the cloakroom, along with their jackets, and Angelien went to buy their tickets.

'Are you ever going to tell me why we've come here?' asked Alex.

Angelien smiled.

'Don't you like surprises?' she said.

'Depends,' said Alex. '*Some* surprises are OK.'

Angelien turned and put her hand on his shoulder.

'Trust me. I think there is a painting here that you will want to see,' she said. 'Come on.'

They walked into a large room. The walls were high and wide. Above them was a kind of walkway. It was all much more modern inside than Alex had expected.

There was a massive wooden model of a sailing ship with a huge cannon laid out horizontally. There seemed to be a military theme to the room, with armour and flintlock pistols and a cabinet of swords.

'They look like samurai swords,' said Alex.

'They are,' said Angelien. 'The Dutch were a super-power in those days. Before you had the British Empire we had colonies all over the world. New York was New Amsterdam first you know.'

'Really?' said Alex.

'Sure,' said Angelien. 'Don't they teach you any-thing in England? The Dutch were especially big in the Far East – hence all the Indonesian restaurants. Van Kampen – who owned the house that became your hotel – made a lot of his money trading with Japan.'

And the next few paintings seemed to illustrate this, with scenes of exotic places. Not that anyone looked happy. There was a gloomy portrait where the whole family looked thoroughly miserable at finding themselves in whatever tropical paradise it depicted.

'This way,' said Angelien, and they climbed a wooden staircase to the upstairs galleries. They walked past still lifes and paintings of tulips. Alex stopped to look at a winter landscape with lots of black-clad figures like beetles on a frozen lake. He spent a long time studying all the little figures and grinned at the bare bottom sticking out of one of the buildings, the comical effect of some kind of primitive toilet.

They passed a painting of figures outside a church, all in black with wide-brimmed hats. The Dutch seemed to be in love with black in those days; practically everyone in these pictures was wearing it.

Alex was beginning to feel that his interest in painting was being pushed to the limits. But he didn't want to show that to Angelien and so he followed and said nothing.

Angelien had moved ahead to stand beside a painting and was beckoning to him to come over. Alex walked slowly towards her. An elderly couple stepped in front of him and blocked his view. The woman turned and saw him coming and there was something about the look on Alex's face that made her tug her husband's arm and pull him away.

Alex stood in front of the painting, mesmerised. It was not large but it had a wide and ornate golden frame around it. In the centre of the painting was a figure standing in a window, the face a pale and smiling mask.

'That mask,' said Alex quietly. 'It looks just like my mask.'

Angelien nodded, clearly waiting for Alex to notice something else.

'And that looks just like the hotel.'

'It *is* your hotel,' said Angelien. 'The part that you are staying in. Spooky, huh?'

Suddenly it was as though the floor was tilting towards the painting ahead of him, and he would stumble and fall into it. It seemed to take an effort of will to stay upright as he struggled against the dizziness.

He felt himself drawn into the painting, leaning forward, his eyes and attention pulled towards the window of the room he knew was his hotel room, and to the strange masked face that looked out at him through the grimy varnish and cracked paint.

The masked figure was a girl, he could now see. The painting showed a night scene, but age had darkened it further. Much of the painting was impenetrable blackness, out of which loomed various figures – figures of children running and playing

– illuminated by a full moon that shone overhead. Alex turned to look at Angelien.

'I know,' said Angelien in response to Alex's baffled expression. 'You can see why I was so surprised when I saw the mask. I had been looking at the painting only two days before.'

Alex looked back at the painting. It was so dark, so gloomy. It seemed to carry the night with it and, just as though he were looking at a real night scene, Alex's eyes strained to adjust to the low light.

'I don't . . .' he began. 'How? How can that be?'

Angelien shrugged and looked back at the picture.

'Honestly, I don't have any explanation,' she said with a shake of her head. 'It's crazy.'

Alex looked at the girl in the painting and it felt as though he was being pulled towards her. He could see her so vividly – every crease in her clothes, every pore on the flesh of her pale arms. He could see her eyes glistening in the shadows in the dark sockets of the mask.

The strange feeling of dread he had experienced in his hotel room returned and gripped his body. His breathing was becoming shorter and his throat seemed to be tightening up as though he was being choked by a powerful hand.

'Alex?' said Angelien. 'Are you OK?'

'I'm fine,' said Alex with a weak smile, rubbing his forehead with the tips of his fingers.

'Sure?' said Angelien.

'I'm OK – really,' said Alex, pulling his eyes from the masked girl with some difficulty and moving across the picture, taking in the full strangeness of it. 'It's so weird.'

'Come,' said Angelien, putting her arm round him. 'Let's go and sit.'

Angelien led Alex out to the stairs they had walked up and they sat down on the top step. Alex felt nauseous and his legs ached as though he had just been for a long run.

'You looked as though you were about to pass out on me,' Angelien said. 'Maybe you shouldn't look so hard.'

Nearby a family hissed angrily to each other. They kept this low volume argument up for a few minutes and then left in a sullen knot, muttering rhythmically with each step of their descent.

The family's mood was mirrored by the weather, which had worsened. Rain was now dribbling down the panes of the windows and the sky was dark and brooding. When Angelien spoke, it was in a near whisper.

'That painting was done by a man called Pieter Graaf,' said Angelien. 'He lived in a house on the opposite side of the canal from where your hotel is now.'

'How do you know?'

'I have been given access to the letters and journals of Pieter Graaf for my research. They were mislabelled and have lain in a box in the university archive ever since they were donated by his family back in the 1880s. I'm very lucky actually. A friend came across them by accident and knew I was researching in this area –'

'But why did he paint my mask?' interrupted Alex.

'I'm still trying to find out what that painting's about. It's a strange picture – unlike the rest of his work.'

'What do you mean?'

'Graaf was a portrait painter mostly. Not a famous one, not Rembrandt or anything, but a successful one all the same. That picture is clearly more than just a painting of the girl.

'He was a young painter on the make,' said Angelien. 'He had come to the city to make his fortune. There were plenty of vain and wealthy merchants here. It was a good move.

'He was the son of wealthy merchants himself, in fact, so he must have found it easy to move in those circles. Amsterdam was the place to be if you wanted to earn your living as a painter. Paintings were seen as really fashionable in the Golden Age. Anyone who was anyone had to have paintings on the wall. They were everywhere – in homes, in shops, in warehouses.

'Graaf was in competition with some of the greatest painters Holland has ever seen, but there was enough work to go round and enough money to pay for it.'

Angelien pulled in her feet to let someone pass.

'He lived pretty well and moved in high society. He seems to have enjoyed himself immensely if half of what is in his journals is true. But he was clearly fascinated with the family who lived opposite.'

'So does that mean you know all about the girl?' said Alex. 'The girl in the painting?'

'Hanna,' said Angelien.

The name seemed to echo round the stairwell and flutter towards Alex's ear to die as a whisper.

'Is that her name?'

But some part of Alex already seemed to know this.

Angelien nodded.

'I do know some things,' she said. 'Quite a lot actually. But I haven't finished reading the journals yet. I've only just been given access to Graaf's journals and his writing is really hard to read a lot of the time.

It's taking for ever to decipher. Plus I've been a bit distracted with babysitting duties, as you know.'

Angelien smiled and Alex smiled back, blushing a little.

'Graaf seems to have been intrigued by the Van Kampens right from the start. He was always on the lookout for new clients and he wasn't going to ignore a rich merchant living right opposite.

'The painter went over to introduce himself and noted that Van Kampen had no wife, that he seemed very strict and severe and, even more surprisingly, that the daughter wore a mask.'

'Did he meet Hanna?' asked Alex.

'No,' said Angelien. 'That's the strange thing. He writes about her for years but never ever seems to physically meet her. Maybe that's why he became so obsessed by her.'

'But why did she wear the mask?' asked Alex. 'Did Graaf find out?'

Angelien nodded.

'Hanna had been badly burned in a fire as a small child. Her face had been horribly disfigured and so she wore that mask at all times and never left the house. She was so horrified by her appearance that she did not want to see it or to have others see it. They allowed no mirrors in the house for fear that Hanna would see her own terrible face.'

Alex thought how strange it was that a young girl like Hanna had worn a mask showing the face of an old woman.

'Do you really think the mask I bought could be the one from the painting?' said Alex. 'The one the girl is wearing?'

'Who knows,' she said. 'Maybe. Anything's possible, right? The mask itself looks like a Japanese *noh* mask – a mask used in Japanese theatre – though I'm no expert. But it makes sense that her father brought it back from Japan.'

'What about her mother?' he said. 'Where was she?'

'Van Kampen told people that she had died, but it seems that wasn't true. She wanted more out of life,' she said.

'What do you mean?' asked Alex.

Angelien smiled.

'Graaf did a bit of asking around and it turns out she had left before they even moved to Amsterdam. She ran away with another man,' said Angelien with a grin. 'And good for her. Van Kampen sounds like a terrible bore.'

Alex scowled.

'Not so good for her daughter,' he said.

'Hey, I'm sorry,' said Angelien, reaching out and touching Alex's hand. 'I wasn't thinking. I've got a big mouth, you know that. I'm sorry, Alex.'

'They always say "run off", don't they?' Alex said after a moment. 'It sounds cool. It sounds like an adventure. But she didn't run off. She just left one day and didn't come back.'

Angelien nodded.

'Yeah,' she said. 'I know.'

Alex had a sudden panic that he was going to cry. He felt his eyes moisten and knew that Angelien must see it. He looked away towards the window.

'Do you see much of her?' said Angelien.

'Why would I?' said Alex.

'She's still your mother,' she said with a smile.

'She *was* my mother,' said Alex. 'She has a new family now. The guy she went off with has kids younger than me.'

'Oh,' said Angelien. 'That must be hard. You must have been very upset.'

Alex leaned forward.

'I hate her! OK? I'm not upset,' he hissed. 'I just hate her.'

Angelien's smile disappeared and Alex muttered, standing up.

'Alex,' said Angelien, reaching out to touch his hand. 'I'm sorry. Hey . . . sit down. Please.'

Alex stood there for a moment, staring at the floor, before slowly sinking back on to the step next to Angelien.

'I never thought I'd be one of those kids,' said Alex finally.

'Which kids?' said Angelien.

'You know,' said Alex. 'Those kids that people look at and say, "It's such a shame." I don't want people to feel sorry for me.'

'But you feel sorry for yourself,' said Angelien.

'Yeah,' said Alex. 'Sometimes I do. I just want everything to be normal. I don't want to have to think about all that stuff.'

Angelien nodded.

'People used to look at me like that when my dad died. I was only little you know.'

'What was he like?' asked Alex.

'Oh he was great,' she said with a grin. 'He was funny and clever. He was handsome too – really handsome, in an old-fashioned kind of way.'

'But you get on OK with your mum, don't you?' asked Alex.

'Sure,' said Angelien. 'But she's been on her own a long time and she deserves to be with someone. Also she might be less weird if she was with someone. Ha!'

Angelien laughed to herself and Alex joined in, just because it felt good to laugh along and Angelien looked so nice when she laughed. But he was also thinking how strange it would be now if their parents did get together and they ended up as step-brother and sister.

'Is she weird then, your mum?' said Alex.

Angelien nodded.

'God, yes,' she said. 'But mostly in a good way. I'm pretty weird myself come to think of it, so maybe I get that from her.'

'You don't seem weird to me,' said Alex.

'Ah, but when you get to know me better,' she said, 'maybe you'll change your mind, huh?'

Alex grinned.

'Maybe,' he said, nodding.

They stayed like that for a moment, looking at each other. Angelien chuckled.

'I feel sorry for Hanna,' said Alex. 'Not much of a life, was it?'

'No,' said Angelien. 'Not much.'

7

Alex strolled along a wall that had postcards and greeting cards arranged for view and for sale in the gift shop. He was inevitably drawn to the far end and to a reproduction of the girl in the mask. The image was so small it was hard to make out any of the details but he still wanted to buy it, if only to confirm what he already felt – that the two masks were identical.

There was a long padded bench next to the post-cards and, after picking two or three more, Alex sat down. A girl was sitting nearby and Alex had the impression that, as he turned to look at her, she had just looked away and was pretending to read a book she had picked up. She was blushing slightly and, while he was looking, she looked up and then back to her book, smiling to herself. Alex frowned.

Angelien appeared at the door of the gift shop and walked over, shaking her hair.

'It's disgusting out there,' she said. 'Why am I so stupid? Smoking is so stupid.'

She sat down, hugging herself.

'I'm freezing!' she said. 'I should have gone and got my coat first. Did you find anything?'

Alex showed her the postcard.

'I thought I'd just get this,' he said.

'That reminds me,' said Angelien.

She walked over to the postcards and came back holding one.

'Let's pay.'

They went over to the till. Alex laid his cards down on the counter. Angelien had chosen a portrait but before he could see it properly it disappeared into a small paper bag with the others. The man at the till reached over and collected the money Angelien had put down.

'Come on,' said Angelien as Alex took his change. 'I have another painting to show you before we go.'

As they turned to walk out, the girl who had been sitting next to him looked over again and didn't look away when Alex glanced over. Angelien followed his gaze and smiled.

Angelien took Alex back towards the gallery with the painting of the masked girl. But instead of turning left to go and see that painting, they turned right and headed through an arched door into another room.

'That girl was totally checking you out,' said Angelien as they walked along.

'What girl?' said Alex.

'In the shop,' said Angelien. 'Don't tell me that you didn't see her because I don't believe you.'

'No she wasn't,' said Alex smiling.

'Absolutely, she was.'

'Anyway,' said Alex. 'She isn't my type.'

'You have a type?' said Angelien with a chuckle.

Alex was trying to think of something to say in reply when Angelien turned and pointed towards a painting on the far side of the gallery. There was a wall of dour portraits of men dressed all in black save for their white lace collars. Angelien headed towards a particular one and stood in front of it waiting for Alex. He recognised it as the postcard Angelien had bought.

'This,' she said, 'is Van Kampen.'

'Hanna's father?'

'The very same. And it was painted by our friend Graaf. Cheerful-looking fellow, huh?' said Angelien, screwing up her face.

Alex frowned. That was an understatement. Even allowing for the fact that none of the people in the portraits were smiling and they all looked as though they had never laughed in their lives; even so – this man looked horribly grim.

'He was a very successful merchant. Not that he was the sort to get much pleasure out of that success. In fact, he would probably have thought the whole idea of pleasure was a little ungodly.'

'Ungodly?' said Alex.

'Well,' said Angelien. 'They liked to make money, those guys, but they worried about getting into heaven too. They didn't want to enjoy it all too much.'

His cold glare seemed to pierce Alex's flesh and he felt his face tingle as though a chill breeze had blown into the room.

Van Kampen was tall and thin. He was dressed in black. Light played along the creases in his sleeves, showing the complex web of embroidery. The clothes may have been dour and black but they were clearly very expensive.

He had white lace gathered at his cuffs and a large round expanse beneath his chin that gave the impression of his head sitting on a dinner plate. The lace was only marginally paler than his skin.

His was a face in which the skull seemed all too easy to discern, the skin stretched tightly across the bone.

Beneath his long, aquiline nose was a moustache

that curled up at the ends. Beneath that were thin, colourless lips. A reddish beard tufted from his long pointed chin, the longest hairs resting against the white lace ruff.

He was standing at an angle to the viewer, not quite side on, not quite face forward, facing a little towards the right, but with his piercing eyes looking straight out.

The left side of Van Kampen's face – the side furthest from Alex – was in shadow and almost merged with the featureless grey wall behind him.

In a morbid echo of Van Kampen's skeletal face, he held, in his left hand, a human skull, which, unlike Van Kampen, turned its eyeless sockets directly at Alex. In his other hand he held a cane.

'It's like a reminder that we all die,' said Angelien, following Alex's gaze. 'It's actually quite common to find a skull in these paintings. They were sort of saying that no matter how rich or successful they were, they were all going to die and be judged.'

'Judged?' said Alex.

'By God,' said Angelien.

'Do you believe that?' said Alex. 'That we get judged by God?'

Angelien shrugged and grinned crookedly.

'I don't know,' she said. 'How about you?'

Alex shook his head.

'Nah,' he said. 'I don't think I believe in anything really.'

'Everyone believes in something,' said Angelien. 'It doesn't have to be God.'

'What do you believe in?' said Alex.

Angelien smiled.

'Me,' she said. 'I believe in me.'

They left the museum and headed out into the rain to catch a tram back into the centre of town.

'Can I ask you something, Alex?' said Angelien as they walked back towards the hotel.

'Yeah,' said Alex.

Angelien paused, seeming to reconsider if it was such a good idea to ask.

'You seem very angry with your mother,' she said. 'Why do you hate her so much?'

Alex sighed.

'I don't really hate her,' he said.

'OK then,' said Angelien. 'Why are you so mad at her?'

'I've told you already,' he said. 'She went off with another man. She left us.'

'I feel like there's something more than that,' said Angelien.

Alex half closed his eyes. A gull circled above the

canal and then dropped to the water with a cackling call.

Alex sighed again.

'She said some stuff, OK?' he said finally.

'Oh?' said Angelien.

'She said Dad was impossible to live with,' continued Alex. 'That he was always getting at her. She said he tried to control her and stuff. But it wasn't like that at all. We were really happy.'

'Maybe your mum was really good at not showing how unhappy she was.'

Alex shook his head.

'No,' he said. 'It was just an excuse so she could go off and start a new life somewhere else and not even think about us.'

Angelien made no reply. They had come to a halt near a bridge and a barge was going past.

'What?' said Alex.

'I didn't say anything,' said Angelien with a shrug.

'Yeah – but I know you want to,' said Alex.

Angelien leaned forward. 'I was going to say that you cannot know how people behave when they are in that kind of relationship. People don't always act like they do with other people. We are sometimes most cruel to the ones we love. It's just part of life.'

'You're saying you think my mum is right? You're saying my dad made her miserable?'

'No, I'm not saying that. I don't really know your dad, Alex,' said Angelien. 'And I don't know your mum at all. But we all have different faces we show to different people, huh?'

Alex turned away, thrust his hands into his pockets and walked towards the side of the canal.

Angelien waited a few moments and then walked up beside him.

'I know this is all none of my business.'

A girl locking up her bike nearby answered her phone and started an animated conversation with the caller, laughing loudly as she walked away.

'I just don't like to see you upset, you know,' said Angelien.

'Yeah?' said Alex with a half smile.

'Yeah,' she said. 'I like you.'

Alex looked back towards the canal. A small boat went past, creating a wake that slapped the side of a houseboat moored nearby.

'Look,' she said. 'When I was a bit younger than you, I had a fight with my dad. It was about something so stupid. He had promised to take me on a trip to France with him and then he backed out. I was so angry with him that I did not speak to him for over two weeks. Not one word.'

She shook her head at the memory of it.

'I was so stubborn,' she said. 'And now – what I wouldn't give for those two weeks with him.'

Alex stared up at the clouds for a moment. A small flock of pigeons scattered across the sky. He looked back at Angelien.

'I got into trouble at school,' he said.

'You don't have to –' began Angelien.

'I want to,' said Alex, looking back towards the water. 'There was this girl. After Mum left. Molly Ryman. I went a bit crazy about her.'

Alex closed his eyes and hung his head.

'So?' said Angelien. 'That doesn't sound such a crime.'

'No, you don't understand. I used to follow her everywhere. When she said she wouldn't go out with me, I was . . . I was . . . I can't really describe it. I sent her all these emails and left loads of messages for her on Facebook until she de-friended me and changed her email, but by then her parents had got involved and told the school . . .'

Alex closed his eyes and a tear rolled down his cheek.

'That's why I'm here,' said Alex. 'My dad thought it might be a good idea to take some time off school. If it hadn't been for the divorce, they might have excluded me for cyber-bullying or harassment or something. I think if my dad wasn't so well known they'd have done it anyway.'

Angelien took him by the shoulders and turned him round to face her, but he could not make eye contact, staring instead at the cobbles between them.

'Thank you for telling me,' she whispered. 'You must not beat yourself up about it, Alex. What you did was wrong, but you are hurting. Anyone can see that.'

She put her arm round him and pulled him close. She felt soft and warm against him and her hair stroked his cheek. The moment seemed to last an hour.

'We cannot always help who we love,' said Angelien. 'Or how we love. But we are in Amsterdam, a city that has known more than its fair share of pain and sadness, and yet here we are. Your sins are very small here. Let's forget about them, huh? What do you say?'

Alex smiled, wiping his face dry with the back of his hand and nodding. As he did so, it began to rain.

'OK then,' she said. 'Back to the hotel, huh?'

Alex nodded as raindrops began to dot the pavement.

8

When he got back to his room, Alex couldn't stop thinking about Angelien. He seemed to feel her hair against his cheek again. Alex wondered what a girl like Angelien saw in someone like Dirk. But girls were weird like that. They said they liked boys who were kind and treated them with respect, and then the next minute they were snogging some creep – like Molly with Carl Patterson.

Alex smiled, imagining the look on Carl Patterson's face if he had seen Alex with Angelien. Or the look on Molly Ryman's face for that matter. But Alex's smile disappeared at the memory of Molly.

The Alex that had pestered Molly Ryman seemed like a different person. He had become hypnotised, obsessed. He felt genuinely sorry for the hurt he had caused but in truth he could barely remember doing anything. It was as though he had been in a kind of trance. He had tried to explain this to his father, but he had said that Alex was just trying to avoid taking responsibility.

Alex pulled out the postcards from the Rijksmuseum and looked at them. They seemed so ordinary compared to the actual paintings. Shrunken to this size, Van Kampen did not seem quite so intimidating.

But even as Alex had that thought, it was as if a window was thrown open on to a winter's night and a cold draught played across his neck and back. He looked at the painting of Hanna at the window and went over to get his mask to compare.

The shape, the eye sockets, the angle of the smile – they all seemed very similar. But at this scale it was hard to be sure. Alex had an idea. He left the cards in his room and headed down to the lobby.

'Excuse me,' he said to the woman on reception. 'Do you have a magnifying glass?'

'I'm sorry?' she said.

'It doesn't matter,' said Alex, realising how strange the request might seem.

'A magnifying glass, is it?' said the manager stepping out from his office. 'We do indeed.'

He rummaged in a drawer and produced a large magnifying glass. He smiled and handed it over to Alex.

'Some of our older customers sometimes forget their glasses and they use this to read the newspaper,' he said. 'I use it myself sometimes. The print is so small these days.'

'Thanks,' said Alex.

'Off to solve a murder?' said the manager.

'Huh?' said Alex.

'The magnifying glass?' said the manager. 'Like your Sherlock Holmes? "Elementary, my dear Watson."'

'Oh,' said Alex with a nod. 'Yeah.'

Alex went back to his room. He lifted the post-card to his face, holding the magnifying glass over it, studying the details of the painting.

The lens seemed to have a magical effect. It not only magnified, it seemed to sharpen the image and throw the detail into startling 3D. The shadows became deep wells of darkness, the mask and the moon the only real points of light in the whole picture. The ghostly children were particularly vivid. Alex moved the glass across to look at Hanna herself.

The masks were identical; Alex could see this now with terrible clarity. There could be no argument. Every detail was the same, every carved wrinkle. So much so, that Alex found looking from the painted mask to his mask and back again was dizzying. It was an impossible degree of detail; impossible and yet there it was.

Alex put the card down and picked up the portrait of Van Kampen, looking into the face of the man who walked these rooms all those centuries ago. His coldness seemed to outlive him; it seemed to have infected this part of the building.

Then Alex noticed the cane he was holding and squinted at the postcard, not quite able to believe what he was seeing. He held the magnifying glass in front of the handle of the cane and, no matter how many times he looked, he was absolutely sure that it was the same as the one hanging from his father's key.

Alex picked up the card showing Hanna again. The vertigo he had felt in the gallery looking at the actual painting now returned as he focused on what Hanna was wearing, finding what he hoped he would not but somehow knew he would.

Alex was aware that he was seeing an impossible amount of detail, as though he was able to climb into the painting and inspect anything he liked.

Sure enough, there on Hanna's dress, beneath the lace collar, was a brooch with a small cameo in the centre. Alex picked up his key and saw the remains of that brooch hanging from it. Looking again, he could see now that the clock that ticked in his room was also ticking in the shadows behind Hanna.

How could this be? It was as if the room, the hotel,

were acting like a magnet, attracting these objects back to the place where they belonged.

Somehow the manager's wife had been an unwitting courier in this process, and now whatever had possessed her to buy these things was working its will on Alex.

Alex peered at the mask on the bed before him. He knew for sure now: this wasn't some replica of the one in the painting; it was the same mask.

'Ready?' said his father as he came through their connecting door.

Alex jumped, fumbling the postcards and dropping one on the floor.

'You should knock,' said Alex, picking them up.

'Why?' said his father. 'What are you up to?'

'Nothing,' said Alex. 'That's not the point.'

'All right,' said his father. 'Don't get all stroppy about it. I'll knock next time, OK?'

Alex grunted and put the postcards on the chest of drawers. His father leaned over and looked at them.

'What are these?' he asked, picking one up and peering at it.

'Just some postcards,' said Alex. 'Angelien took me to the Rijksmuseum today.'

'Really?' said his father, his eyebrows arching. 'I wouldn't have thought that was your thing.'

Alex's mind was still struggling to cope with the idea of the former contents of the room being drawn back somehow.

'I'm interested in loads of things you don't know about,' said Alex. 'Just because it isn't World War Two. Anyway, Angelien makes it interesting.'

'Oh,' said his father, nodding his head and smiling. 'I see.'

'What's that supposed to mean?' said Alex.

'Nothing,' said his father. 'Are you OK?'

'Me? Yeah,' said Alex. 'Sorry.'

'That's OK. Come on. Let's go. I'm starving.'

The restaurant was in a small street off the Prinsengracht and was small and cave-like. There were very few tables but all were occupied, mainly by earnest-looking couples lit by the glow of tea lights. At the far end of the room, he could see Saskia waving. Angelien turned to face them, smiling.

'Hello again,' said Saskia. 'Sit down, sit down. They'd put us over by the door but there was such a chilly draught I got them to move us over here.'

'Any further,' said Alex's father. 'And we'd be in the kitchen cooking the food.'

'Nonsense,' said Saskia. 'I love being near the kitchen in a restaurant. I love to smell all the aromas and hear the sizzle of the food being cooked.'

She said these words looking straight at Alex and he smiled, not really knowing what to say in response.

'How did you enjoy yourself today?' said Saskia. 'I hear my daughter took you to the Rijksmuseum. Do you like art, Alex?'

Alex cast a quick glance at his father.

'Yeah,' he said. 'I do like paintings. I like a bit more colour though.'

Saskia chuckled.

Alex's mind was pulled back to the postcards. He needed to talk to Angelien.

'They can be a little sombre, it's true,' Saskia said. 'But if you like colour you should get Angelien to take you to the Van Gogh museum, Alex. Do you like Van Gogh?'

'That's the way they pronounce Van Gogh's name here,' said Alex's father, seeing his son's puzzled face. 'Van "Hoch" – like Lo*ch* Ness.'

'It's not how we pronounce it here,' said Saskia frowning. 'It is how his name should be pronounced. Not "Van Goff" or "Van Go". It is not so hard to pronounce a man's name correctly, is it?'

'Wine?' said the waitress as she came over.

'Oh – whatever you're drinking, Saskia,' said Alex's father.

'Another glass of Sangiovese,' said Saskia. 'And what about you, Alex. Coke? Juice?'

'No thanks,' said Alex. 'Water's fine. I'm really thirsty.'

The waitress handed them the menus and pointed to the specials of the day on a large blackboard nearby. Alex peered at the board, looking for words he understood.

'Jeremy tells me you bought a mask in the antiques market?' said Saskia, when they had ordered their food.

'Yes,' said Alex, glancing at Angelien.

Alex's father sighed and shook his head.

'What were you thinking of, letting Alex buy that thing, Angelien?' he said without looking up from the menu. 'What a waste of money.'

'Actually,' said Angelien. 'I'm not an expert but I think Alex may have got a bargain. It looks like it might be a very old Japanese *noh* mask. I think it may be worth a lot more than twenty euros.'

Alex's father smiled and shook his head.

'You don't think so?' said Angelien.

'No,' said his father. 'I would bet twenty euros it's a fake.'

'You haven't even looked at it, Dad,' said Alex. 'How would you know?'

'Historians just have a nose for this kind of thing,' he said with a smile.

Angelien frowned and pouted her lips but made no reply.

'Anyway,' said Saskia, trying to lighten the mood. 'Sometimes it's hard to explain why we buy such things. Sometimes they just seem irresistible. Did the person who sold it to you tell you something interesting about it?'

'No,' said Alex. 'I don't know why I bought it really.'

Alex's father sighed and shook his head again.

'You could always try to take it back,' he said.

'No!' said Alex loudly enough to attract the attention of the diners around them. He was surprised at the vehemence of his own voice.

'OK,' said his father firmly. 'Calm down.'

'Oh, leave him alone, Jeremy,' said Saskia. 'They wouldn't take it back anyway, would they, Angelien?'

Angelien shook her head.

'No chance,' she said.

Alex's father opened his mouth to say something else but Saskia jumped in ahead of him and began telling a story about an Italian restaurant she had been to in Rome where the kitchen had caught fire. Alex caught Angelien's eye and smiled to himself.

Talk of the mask put Alex on edge once more and he forced himself to concentrate on the conversation around him to stop himself thinking about it. It was too weird.

'Well that was excellent,' said Alex's father when they had all finished.

'It really was,' said Alex.

He had eaten more than he had intended to and his stomach felt as though it was about to burst. Saskia could not have looked more pleased had she cooked the meal herself.

'Have you had enough?' she asked.

'I have,' said Alex's father. 'I'm stuffed.'

'Me too,' said Alex.

'But don't let us stop you,' said Alex's father.

'No, no, no,' said Saskia with a chuckle. 'We have to watch our weight, don't we, Angelien?'

Angelien looked at Alex and shook her head witheringly. Saskia ignored her and waved to the waitress and asked for the bill.

'You must let me pay,' said Alex's father, grabbing the bill as it was put down on the table.

'No, no –'

'We insist,' said Alex's father. 'Don't we, Alex?'

Alex grinned.

'Yeah, we do,' said Alex.

'Well if you are sure,' said Saskia. 'Thank you.'

'Thanks,' said Angelien.

'Nonsense,' said Alex's father, handing his card to the waitress. 'It's the least we could do.'

9

A large group of raucous and drunken Englishmen lumbered by as Alex and his father walked back to the hotel. Alex could hear them swearing and laughing, their harsh voices slapping against the buildings. It was worse somehow, being able to understand them. There were groups of drunken men all over Amsterdam, but only the English ones made him feel embarrassed.

'It's not too boring for you?' asked his father. 'All this socialising with people you don't really know? I'm sorry we haven't had more time together.'

'That's OK, Dad,' said Alex. 'And I'm sorry about the stuff at school. I know you were ashamed of me and everything.'

His father came to a sudden halt and grabbed Alex's arm. 'I was never *ashamed* of you, Alex,' he said. 'I was worried about you, annoyed at you even – but ashamed? No.'

'Thanks, Dad,' said Alex. 'I know I've caused a lot of trouble. I'm really sorry.'

His father put his arms round him and hugged him.

'We'll get by, won't we, eh?' he said. 'They try to put us down but we get back up again, don't we?'

'Yeah,' said Alex.

'It's been a rough time for us both,' said his father.

'I know, Dad.'

'Even so, I know it must be a bit awkward with Saskia and Angelien.'

'No, Dad,' said Alex. 'It's fine.'

And it was fine. He surprised himself at how relaxed he felt around Saskia and Angelien after such a short amount of time.

'She's not banging on too much about the Golden Age, I hope?' he asked. 'Angelien? Some historians can be real bores about their subject.'

Alex smiled to himself. His father clearly didn't count his own obsession with the Second World War as part of this problem.

'I find all that stuff about merchants and guilds a bit dry to be honest,' said his father. 'Oh, I know we are supposed to be fascinated by Amsterdam back then, but when you are a historian some things grab you and others don't. It's hard to explain.'

'Actually . . .' began Alex.

He wanted to tell his father about the paintings and about the strangeness surrounding the mask but he couldn't bring himself to do it.

'Yes?' said his father.

'Nothing,' said Alex.

His father always scoffed at anything that smacked of the supernatural. So did Alex normally, for that matter.

Alex's mother had a much more open mind on that kind of thing and his father would give her a hard time about it. For the first time in a long while Alex found himself wishing that he could tell his mother about this, knowing in his heart that she wouldn't make him feel foolish for speaking about it.

'Well don't be bullied, Alex,' said his father. 'There are all kinds of fascinating aspects to Amsterdam and they don't all revolve around the Golden Age and merchants and guilds. When I'm free, we'll go to the Anne Frank museum. We can't have you come to Amsterdam and not go there.'

The reflections of the hotel and the houses either side of it were swaying back and forth on the black waters of the canal. Lights were on in the windows and these too moved gently on the surface, doubling the effect and making the whole street look brighter and more cheerful than Alex had ever seen it by daylight.

The receptionist gave them their keys and they climbed the stairs to their rooms, saying goodnight on the landing. Alex opened his door, turned on the lights and slumped down on to his bed. As he pulled off his jacket and felt his mobile phone in his pocket, he thought about calling his mother.

But as soon as he touched his phone he knew that he could not call her as if everything was cool again. Everything wasn't cool. Not by a long way.

Alex got into bed and reached over for his book. He was reading *The Big Sleep*. His father had recommended it and normally that would put him off, but he had recently seen the film and liked it and he thought he would give the book a go.

He liked the way the private investigator Philip Marlowe talked and the way he handled the daughter of his rich client. Alex wished he could be like that. Marlowe never seemed to let people get the better of him. He always seemed to know the right thing to do, the right thing to say. There were a few people he wouldn't mind punching on the nose either.

But Alex was never going to be like that, he knew. He was going to be like his father and maybe that wasn't so bad. Women like kind men, his mother had told him once; they liked gentle men.

Maybe they did, thought Alex. Some women did, probably. But what about Carl Patterson? There was nothing kind about him. Molly didn't seem to mind. And Dirk? How kind or gentle was he?

Alex had a sneaking suspicion that women also liked tough men – men like Philip Marlowe. Being kind was OK as far as it went, but sometimes it seemed like weakness.

He found his place in *The Big Sleep* and settled down beside the lamp to read. But he could not concentrate. Angelien's smiling face in the Rijksmuseum filled his thoughts. It loomed large in his mind, as though she was standing improbably close, her lips close to his face.

But though this image was a very attractive one, frustratingly, it kept slipping out of focus and the background would sharpen until it was revealed in hyper detail. Past her ear, over her shoulder, he found himself straining to look at the paintings.

As his eyes moved down the page, so his mind would wander back to the Rijksmuseum and the paintings. He realised that he wasn't taking anything in, so he replaced the bookmark and set it down on the table next to his bed.

He looked across at the chest of drawers where he kept the mask. He looked at the clock and once again returned to the Rijksmuseum and the strange moonlit painting of the girl and the children in the street. The image of it had infested his mind. It was more than a memory of a painting; it had become more like a thought or a memory of something he had actually experienced himself.

Alex got out of bed and padded quietly across to the chest of drawers. He could hear the soft rasp of the clock and the distant murmur of the traffic in the city centre.

He picked the mask up and turned it over in his hands. The inside was smooth and probably made smoother still by years of being worn. Alex ran his fingers along the wood and thought of Hanna and her ruined face and the fire-scarred flesh of it touching the surface as his fingertips now did.

Again he had the sudden, disturbing sensation that he wasn't alone in the room. He knew if he turned he would see nothing there. It was worse somehow – knowing there was nothing there and yet knowing, just as certainly, that there was.

'Why did you want me to buy this?' said Alex. 'What am I supposed to do with it?'

Alex's voice sounded loud in the silence, even though he spoke in little more than a whisper. He had a horrible feeling that he would hear a reply, but none came. He breathed a long sigh of relief.

He held the mask up to his face and peered

through the eyeholes. The view was unexpectedly dark, as if the holes were somehow blocking out the light. He could barely see a thing except the faint glimmer of light catching the clock on the chest of drawers.

Alex lowered the mask and the light flooded back in. He heard a noise outside and wandered over to the window.

Looking out, Alex could see a man and a woman walking beside the canal. The woman was walking away quickly. The man called after her and she turned, her face catching the light from the lamp nearby. She stopped, putting her hand to her face.

The man approached slowly. Alex could hear his voice, though he couldn't understand the language. But he could hear the apologetic, pleading tone.

The woman let him approach and he reached out to touch her arm. But she pulled away, turning on him fiercely and shouting, her voice breaking as she began to sob.

The man stood, head bowed for a little while, but then he reached out again. This time the woman didn't pull away and the man moved closer. They embraced and kissed and held each other for a few long moments before moving off again, hand in hand. The patter of their footfalls became steadily more distant and quiet.

Once again Alex felt a little self-conscious at spying on such an intimate moment and, looking away, became aware once more of the mask in his hand. He put the mask to his face and looked through the window again.

As before, the view was darker but he found that his eyes did get used to it after a few moments. But as they did adjust to the gloom, Alex saw that the view was not simply darker, it was different. The effect was unsettling, disorientating: he felt himself leaning as though the floor had moved, as though the room was now a shipboard cabin, and the ship was riding a large swell.

He reached out and placed his hand on the wall for support. How cold it felt. He looked out of the window. There was a cold blue sheen to the whole scene.

The canal-side was devoid of cars and the parking places that would have been crowded with them were not there. The view was recognisably the same and yet utterly different.

The shops on the opposite side of the canal were not there. Their warm yellow lights no longer twinkled in the ripples and eddies of the canal below.

It wasn't simply that they had closed up or suffered some power cut – they were not there. The illuminated signage, the wide windows – it was all gone, replaced by the weathered wood of warehouse doors. It couldn't be, he knew that – and yet it was.

A pulse hammered in his temple as he tried to make sense of it. And then he was aware of movement out of the corner of his eye. Dark shapes were moving in the shadows of those dark canal-side streets.

Then out into the pools of moonlight came the children, scampering along the cobbles. It was just like the painting of Hanna in her mask. He looked up. Even the big, bone-coloured moon was there.

Somehow, some way, he was seeing the past through the mask. He was seeing the world that she saw when she stood at her window. Alex knew that there was more to it, even, than that. He felt that he wasn't just seeing what Hanna was seeing, but seeing *as* Hanna – seeing with a combination of her mind and his.

The children ran and skipped and played leap-frog. One moment they appeared to be moving in slow motion, the next they seemed to flicker across the scene like blue flames or scuttle with the horrible efficiency of insects.

But, slowly or swiftly, their destination became clear as they gathered one by one in the street outside the hotel. They huddled as though in deep discussion, though Alex could hear no sound. Then all at once they turned their faces to look straight at him.

Alex snatched the mask from his face, blinking against the welcome street lights and electric glare that burst in on him from every side.

He walked to the chest of drawers, replaced the mask and put on his bedside light. He got into bed, closing his eyes immediately, not casting even the swiftest glance towards the hidden mask.

10

Alex woke and looked around the room, blearily at first, sleep still clouding his mind. But then the memory of what he had seen through the mask came back and he sat bolt upright, looking over to the chest and to the mask he knew was secreted in the drawer.

He took faltering breaths and his heart thumped. The vision of the world glimpsed through the mask swept back in on him with horrible suddenness, like a smothering black blanket.

The ghostly images punctured the mundane reality of his hotel room with their inky shadows and wash of moon glow: those pale children gathered in the street outside his hotel.

Alex got out of bed and walked to the window, hesitating before pulling back the curtain. The modern world was mercifully restored. All was as it should be.

The shops were already open across the canal. A delivery van was unloading. A cyclist pinged her bell as she rode past, white headphone leads against long black hair.

Alex rubbed his eyes and pulled his fingers down his face, dragging the sides of his mouth down as he did so. He looked at the drawer where he kept the mask, but only briefly. Then he got dressed.

At breakfast, Alex's father asked him if he was all right, saying that he looked pale. He told him that he hadn't slept well, that there was an argument in the street outside.

'Really?' said his father. 'Never heard a thing. I was out like a light. You can always go back to bed and have a lie-in. I'm sure Angelien won't mind.'

'No,' said Alex, blinking hard, finding it hard to concentrate surrounded by the noise of breakfast diners. He seemed to hear every scrape of knives on plates, every spoon rattling in a cup, as though it was amplified through giant headphones. 'I want to see her. There's something I need to talk to her about.'

Alex's father smiled and raised his eyebrows.

'You and she are getting very pally,' he said.

Alex shrugged.

'S'pose,' he said. 'Is that all right?'

'Course it is,' said his father with a chuckle. 'It's great that you two have hit it off so well.'

'We're just friends,' said Alex.

His father frowned.

'I never doubted it,' he said.

It was Alex's turn to frown.

'What's that supposed to mean?' said Alex.

'There is a bit of an age difference.'

'Not that much,' said Alex, blushing.

His father smiled, half closing his eyes. It was a smile Alex knew well and hated.

'Saskia is older than you,' said Alex. 'You don't seem to mind.'

'Don't let Saskia hear you say that! Anyway, that's a bit different, Alex,' said his father. 'We met when we were both adults. What is all this? You haven't got a crush on Angelien –'

Alex clamped his hands over his ears.

'No!' he said. 'God!'

An elderly couple nearby turned and stared.

'OK, OK,' said his father with a frown. 'That's enough, Alex.'

Alex chewed on the inside of his bottom lip and said nothing.

'No one says "crush", Dad,' said Alex eventually. 'And I haven't got one anyway.'

'Well that's all right then,' said his father.

What did his father know anyway? Why was it so weird to think there might be something between him and Angelien? Not that there was. But was it so far-fetched?

His father had hardly spoken to Angelien. More to the point he had no idea what Alex was like now. His father still saw him as a little boy. He probably always would.

'I'm not a kid any more,' said Alex.

'I know that, Alex,' said his father with a sigh. 'I know that all too well.'

'This is about what happened at school, isn't it?' said Alex. 'You say you're OK about it but –'

'I did not say I was "OK" about it, Alex,' said his father. 'I said I understood that you have been going through a lot. We both have. But the fact remains that you caused a lot of people a lot of aggravation, Alex. I don't want any nonsense while I'm here.'

'But –'

'Alex,' said his father firmly. 'I mean it. You need to grow up.'

Alex hung his head. His father put his hands to his face as though he were praying for guidance.

'Alex,' he said more softly. 'I'm sorry I haven't spent more time with you. All this stuff at the publishers – well it could be really important. If it goes well, then we could be going to New York sooner than we thought.'

'Really?' said Alex.

His father had been promising to take him to New York for years.

'Really,' said his father.

Alex smiled.

'This is potentially a big deal, Alex,' said his father. 'They are talking about me narrating the documentary myself. That would be pretty cool, huh? Your dad on TV? Maybe the BBC? The History Channel? So see if you can just get through the next few days without causing me any problems. Is that possible?'

Alex sighed.

'All right, Dad,' said Alex. 'I get the message. I won't be any trouble. I promise.'

Alex came out of the lift and saw Angelien sitting on her own by the window. A faint beam of milky light had placed a glowing halo around her.

Alex was rooted to the spot for a moment, staring, transfixed at Angelien's golden hair. Then he noticed that the manager who was standing nearby was smiling at him and he walked on.

'Hey, Alex,' said Angelien brightly. 'You OK?'

'Yeah,' he said with a sigh. 'My dad was just giving me a lecture.'

Angelien rolled her eyes.

'Oh, parents,' she said. 'They are so annoying, aren't they?'

'Sometimes. How are you anyway?' said Alex.

Angelien gave him a funny look and then smiled.

'I'm very well. Thank you for asking,' she said.

Alex smiled. For some reason he could think of nothing else to say.

'Shall we go?'

'Sure,' said Angelien.

They left the hotel and began to walk along the canal. Alex was trying to find the right moment to talk to Angelien about the things from the painting being part of the hotel and about the mask. While he was still framing the words in his mind, Angelien broached the subject herself.

'I had a chance to read more of the journal last night,' she said.

'Anything interesting?' asked Alex.

Angelien nodded and continued.

'Something pretty weird actually. There was a series of plagues that hit Amsterdam in the seventeenth century,' she said. 'You probably know about the one that they had in London just before the fire in 1666 . . .'

'The Great Fire of London?' said Alex.

Angelien nodded.

'Yes. Before that there was a plague here in Amsterdam – the Black Death, you know.'

'And did the plague kill Hanna?'

'No,' said Angelien. 'But it did kill many other children in Amsterdam. At least she was safe inside. A lot of people died.'

Alex nodded, trying to imagine the scene and, somehow, it didn't seem as hard as it might. The modern additions to the streets and canals seemed now more tissue-thin and were easily imagined away.

Angelien's dance-track ringtone started up.

'Dirk,' she said, looking at Alex and then turning away.

Alex couldn't understand what Angelien was saying but he could tell from the tone that she was annoyed. Angelien ended the call and stuffed the phone back into her jacket pocket. She looked at the sky and sighed.

'Men are such liars,' she said, turning to Alex. 'That's why you like all that fantasy stuff – all those computer games and stupid books. You live in a fantasy world.'

Alex was both a little annoyed to be lumped in with Dirk and a little pleased to be included by Angelien in the category of 'men'.

'Not all men are liars,' said Alex.

Angelien muttered under her breath.

'What was I saying?' she said.

'You were telling me about the plague,' said Alex.

Angelien nodded.

'Yes,' she said. 'I was going to tell you how the plague is connected with the painting of Hanna.'

'Yeah?' said Alex.

'Graaf went into some detail about that picture and why he painted it,' said Angelien.

'Oh?' said Alex. 'I've got something to tell you about the painting myself.'

'You have?' said Angelien.

'You first,' said Alex. 'What did he say?'

Angelien took out a pack of cigarettes and put one in her mouth. Alex leaned forward and took it from her lips and threw it in the canal.

'What the –'

'You shouldn't smoke,' said Alex with a grin. 'It's bad for you. I'm going to help you give up.'

'It's none of your damned business what I do!' she snapped. 'Who the hell do you think you are? Huh? Huh?'

Angelien turned her back to lean over the railing and shouted angrily at the canal. Alex had been totally unprepared for her reaction and simply stared ahead open-mouthed.

'I'm sorry,' said Alex. 'I –'

Angelien shook her head, calming herself a little.

'Don't ever do that again,' she said, quietly.

'OK,' said Alex.

He was determined not to cry and yet tears were stinging his eyes. Angelien took a deep breath.

'Don't start crying on me,' she said. 'Damn it!'

Alex did not know what to do and stood as still as a statue waiting to see what Angelien would do next. After a moment she took a deep breath and took a long look at him as though seeing him for the first time.

'Don't do that again, Alex, OK?' she said quietly.

'OK,' said Alex. 'I'm sorry.'

Angelien turned and leaned on the railing, staring down the canal. Alex didn't know what to do. He wondered if he was meant to go. Maybe he should just leave and go back to the hotel. He thought about saying something but he felt sure that whatever he said would make things worse.

After a few moments Angelien shook her hair and began talking again as though nothing had happened.

'Back to our friend, Pieter Graaf the painter,' she said. 'It seems that he became fascinated with the girl and –'

'Sorry,' said Alex.

Angelien forced a smile.

'OK. Enough sorrys.'

She took a breath.

'And I shouldn't have yelled,' she said. 'I have a

bad temper. That's something you were going to find out sooner or later. Friends? OK?'

Alex smiled weakly. Angelien began again.

'He became fascinated with Hanna and wanted to know more about her. He spoke to the servants who looked after her, paid them to tell him what had happened before they arrived in Amsterdam. Some of this I've told you already . . .'

Angelien licked her lips.

'Well?' said Alex. 'What else have you found out?' He could see that there was something. Angelien smiled a crooked smile as though she could hardly believe herself what she was about to say.

'Graaf was told that Hanna claimed she could see the ghosts of the children who had died in the plague. The children she had not been allowed to play with who were now deep in the ground.'

'Ghosts?' said Alex, his voice faltering. 'What?'

'Yes,' said Angelien. 'Creepy, huh?'

Alex's stomach seemed to lurch as though he was coming down quickly on a swing. The view from his window the night before came back to him with startling speed and vividness.

'Hey?' said Angelien. 'You OK? You look like you've seen a ghost yourself.'

'I'm . . . OK . . . What else . . .'

'Well,' she continued. 'I was wrong about Graaf

never meeting Hanna because he seems to have talked to her about this himself.

'It was when he was painting Van Kampen's portrait. Van Kampen had to leave on urgent business and Hanna wandered through as he was packing his things away.

'Graaf says that after initially saying nothing, and just standing and watching him from the doorway, Hanna did begin to talk and Graaf asked her whether it was true that she saw ghost children from her window.

'Hanna said that it was true and she seemed more than happy to talk about the whole thing until a servant walked in.' Angelien laughed and shook her head.

'Graaf just doesn't seem to understand that kids make things up, and they did it back then just like they do it now,' she continued. 'The painter just seems to have swallowed her story whole and never questioned it. People were more gullible in those days but this was an educated man. It's amazing really.'

Alex opened his mouth to speak, but Angelien continued.

'Kids don't make the same distinction between imagination and reality that adults do,' said Angelien. She shook her head ruefully. 'Or at least *some* kids, huh?'

She smiled at Alex. His brief spell of being a 'man' was over. He was back to being a 'kid'. But he knew he didn't want to be seen as one of those kids who couldn't tell the real world from the made up. He knew he didn't want to look foolish in Angelien's eyes.

'But you were going to tell me something about the painting,' she said.

'It was nothing,' said Alex. 'I had an idea but it was stupid . . .'

'OK,' said Angelien with a chuckle. 'If you're sure. You hungry?'

'A bit, yeah,' said Alex.

'You want some *frites*?' said Angelien. 'Chips?'

Alex nodded.

'OK,' said Alex.

The area was becoming increasingly seedy and the atmosphere was complemented by the stench coming from the garbage truck that seemed to be following them down the street.

Angelien stopped at a kiosk and ordered two paper cones full of chips. Alex turned his nose up a little at the creamy splodge on top of them.

'What's that?' he asked.

'Mayonnaise,' said Angelien.

Alex screwed his face up and Angelien laughed.

'You Brits always do that – but trust me, it works. Go on, taste it.'

After a moment's hesitation, Alex tried one of the chips. Not only were they very good chips, but Angelien was right – the mayonnaise was delicious. Alex grinned.

'You see?' said Angelien. 'Good, huh?' She patted her stomach. 'Not so good for the waistline though.'

'I don't like skinny girls,' said Alex with a shrug.

'Ha!' said Angelien. 'You're saying I'm fat.'

Alex coughed on the chip he was eating.

'No!' he said. 'I – I just meant . . .'

Angelien laughed again and slapped him on the arm.

'I'm messing with you. Come on – let's get a drink before you dig yourself into a deeper hole. I know a really nice café not far from here.'

11

Angelien set off towards a narrow alleyway lined with shop windows. Or at least that was what Alex took them for. He was halfway along before he realised that in each window there was a female figure standing, almost naked save for some very small pieces of underwear. Alex had thought they were dummies, until he saw one of them move.

Angelien made no comment and looked neither left nor right, but walked through, seemingly oblivious. Alex tried to do the same. They emerged into a much wider street and Angelien walked towards a café with a bench and some folding metal chairs outside it.

'I'm going to have an orange juice,' said Angelien. 'It's fresh. You want one?'

'Yeah, thanks,' said Alex.

Angelien went inside and ordered and then came back, sat down and took out a pack of cigarettes. She put one in her mouth, looked at Alex, sighed and put it back in the pack.

The street was a quiet one, except for the odd cyclist and occasional pedestrian: tourists mainly, it seemed. One man walked by, dragging a case on wheels noisily behind him, stopping to look at a map before continuing on his way.

'That way is De Waag,' Angelien said, pointing down the street after the tourist. 'It was a gatehouse to the old city. Produce was weighed there. Criminals were executed there too and then carved up by surgeons in the anatomy theatre inside.'

Angelien pointed her thumb in the other direction.

'Or they might be taken out to the Volewijk to hang from a pole until they rotted; a horrible warning to those arriving by sea.

'Where the Central Station is now there was the harbour where the bigger merchant ships would anchor. Can you imagine it? There would have been a whole forest of masts. Small boats would ferry the merchandise ashore. But smaller ships would sail straight up the Damrak and drop their goods at the houses of the merchants who –'

'Angelien?' interrupted Alex as the waitress handed them their orange juices.

'What is it?' she said.

'Those women?' said Alex, looking back towards the alleyway they had walked through. 'The women in those shop windows. What's that about?'

Angelien sighed and waved her hand about, a small shower of ash fluttering down from her cigarette and an ash-grey pigeon took to the air nearby.

'It's so embarrassing,' she said. 'But there you go.'

'What?' said Alex.

'They are prostitutes, Alex,' said Angelien, stirring her orange juice with her straw and taking a sip.

'Prostitutes?' said Alex.

'Oh dear,' said Angelien with a smile. 'Have I shocked you?'

'No,' said Alex, smiling and trying to sound relaxed. 'I know about stuff like that.'

In fact, Alex's father had told him a little bit about the red light district. It had just come as a bit of a surprise to actually be there.

Anglelien nodded.'They stand in those windows like they were fridges or TVs,' she said. 'They are for sale. It is a shop selling women. What do you think about that?'

'It's horrible,' said Alex. 'I can't believe it's allowed.'

Angelien shrugged.

'But it is.'

Alex asked if there was a toilet and Angelien pointed to the back of the café. There was a large

119

mirror above the wash basin. Alex looked at himself as he washed his hands, cocking his head and peering at his face as though it belonged to someone else, remembering that Angelien had called him good-looking. He had never thought of himself as good-looking. Maybe he was. He stood back from the mirror and flicked his hair.

He wished he had told her about the mask, but how could he? She would think he was making it up. She would think he was a stupid little kid. At best, she would think he had dreamt it. Maybe he had. It certainly seemed preferable at that moment to thinking that he had looked through the eyes of a dead girl and seen ghost children.

Angelien was paying as Alex appeared at her side and they began to walk back towards the alleyway. Two policemen on mountain bikes cycled by, handguns on their hips. Angelien's phone pinged as she walked towards him. She looked at it and then stuffed it back in her pocket.

'Dirk again,' she said.

'What do you see in him anyway?' said Alex.

'That's none of your business actually,' said Angelien, frowning.

'It's just that – well, he doesn't seem very nice and –'

'Don't be so quick to judge people, Alex. I know he seems like a jerk sometimes, but he has had a really difficult life. I see a different Dirk. He can be so sweet sometimes.'

Alex nodded unconvinced.

'How did you meet him?' he asked.

'The pancake house,' she said. 'He used to work there too.'

When they entered the alleyway, he did not want to look in the windows and faced doggedly ahead, but he was all too aware of the blurred shapes of the women either side of him. He tried to concentrate on the back of Angelien's head and nothing else.

Once out of the alleyway they walked over the canal across a little bridge and stood looking up at the high walls and lead roof and sharp spires of a church – the Oude Kerk.

An unpleasant smell drifted towards Alex's nostrils and he turned to see what he realised was an open-air urinal: a kind of curved metal shield covered the user from knees to shoulders only.

'That's disgusting,' said Alex, screwing up his face.

Angelien laughed.

'It's better than pissing in the street,' she said.

'That *is* pissing in the street,' said Alex. 'It's just doing it behind a bit of metal.'

They walked into a small square and Alex took some photographs looking up at the jagged roofline. They walked on into a narrow alleyway. Alex was trying to frame another shot when a loud tapping made him turn round. There was one of the half-naked women in a window grinning at him and raising her eyebrows.

Angelien stepped forward and banged on the window with the flat of her hand. She pulled Alex away and yelled towards the woman. As they walked away, a group of women shouted at them from the doorway and Angelien stopped and turned round, shouting back at them. Alex may not have understood Dutch but he knew that it was a pretty foul-mouthed exchange. By the time they reached the canal, Angelien was flushed in the face but Alex could see that it was not embarrassment, but anger.

'Everyone thinks we are all cool with this stuff,' said Angelien. 'But it stinks. It is all so . . .'

She waved her hands around struggling to find the right words in English and fired off another volley of Dutch, making an old man on a barge nearby clap his hands and smile.

'All ports are a little bit sleazy,' she said turning to Alex. 'But it's too much – it brings in all these idiots.'

She nodded to a group of guffawing men across the canal who were pointing at one of the women in the windows and shouting. Alex could hear by their voices they were Irish.

'Amsterdam is a beautiful city,' she said. 'She's my home and I love her. Do you understand? No matter what. But sometimes she makes me angry, you know?'

'Yeah,' said Alex.

Angelien reached over and hugged him.

'You're a nice boy, Alex,' she said, her lips so close to his ear that he could feel her breath. 'Come on – let's go in.'

They walked towards the entrance. The sky above was a great bubbling mass of cloud, like balls of grey wool, each a slightly different hue to the one beside it. Thunder rumbled in the distance.

Stepping into the Oude Kerk was startling. Outside the building looked dark and gloomy; inside the ceilings soared high above them on towering columns and huge windows made it seem brighter inside than out.

It was quiet too. The contrast with the streets around the church could not have been more radical. There was a stillness here that seemed as though it was borrowed from another age.

The floor was uneven and flagged with what Alex quickly realised were tombstones. They were inscribed with a number in a sequence, many with other curious marks like little diagrams.

In the centre of the church there was an area of seats and private boxed-in pews with names written in gold paint on the doors. Some of these boxed-in pews were at the foot of columns. There was a pulpit attached to one column with a roof and a staircase with a coiling brass handrail. Brass chandeliers hung on long chains from the high wooden ceiling.

Alex followed Angelien through a carved wooden screen and into the choir stalls. At the back was a row of misericords, the small wooden seats for choir boys, lifted to show the carvings beneath.

'I love them,' said Angelien pointing to the carvings. 'Do you have these in England?'

Alex nodded.

'My mother always used to show me these when I was a kid,' he replied. 'Whenever we would go into a cathedral, she would always head for the choir stalls and be lifting up the seats to check if they had any carvings.'

Angelien passed him the guide they had picked up at the entrance. 'This explains some of them, but a lot of them they don't have any idea about. Sometimes it just looks like the carver was having fun.'

Alex checked the carvings against the diagram in the guide and saw that the misericord showed a man banging his head against a brick wall.

Nearby there was a carving of a man squatting down, coins coming out of his bare backside. 'Money doesn't fall out of my arse,' said the guide by way of explanation.

Alex laughed loudly and a couple who had just walked in scowled at him. Angelien stood next to him and whispered in his ear.

'It's a bit like "Money doesn't grow on trees",' she said.

'I prefer this version,' said Alex.

'It's certainly to the point, huh?' she said with a smile. 'But follow me.'

Angelien stepped through the door at the other side of the choir stall and headed towards a large stained-glass window that Alex realised now was made up of fragments. He stared up into the faces of sullen-looking angels.

Turning to see where Angelien was going, Alex noticed there was a grave slab with the name Saskia carved into it. Angelien stopped and Alex stood alongside her.

'She was Rembrandt's wife,' said Angelien. 'You saw some of his paintings in the Rijksmuseum – remember?'

Alex nodded.

'It's beautiful, isn't it?' said Angelien. 'Just her name spelled out in those big letters.'

Angelien walked on.

'Is it OK to take photos?' asked Alex.

'Sure,' said Angelien.

Alex took his camera out of his bag and took photographs of the tombstones, the misericords and the stained glass and the huge pipe organ and the painted ceiling.

An older man in skinny jeans was studying the tombstones intently, bending over to photograph them. After taking a few more photographs Alex watched him walk away and take a notebook out of his bag and start writing.

Alex looked at the floor himself. The tombstone at his feet was badly worn but he could clearly make out that it showed the body of a man laid out with worms squirming out of his flesh. Next to it was one that had a skull, dust gathering in its eye sockets.

Angelien took her iPhone out of her pocket and after a little tapping and scrolling showed Alex a web page with a diagram of all the tombs in the church.

'Clever, huh?'

As she ran the cursor over it, names appeared next to each tomb.

'So the one at your feet is seventy-eight,' said Angelien, turning away. 'That means that – one, two, three – this one is the tomb of our friend Graaf.'

'Really?' said Alex.

The painter's tombstone was quite decorative.

Alex wondered if he had designed it himself. There was a motif at the bottom which he thought was another skull, but as he leaned in he could see it was actually a mask – and not just any mask. It was *the* mask; the mask that Hanna wore when he had painted her at the window. Angelien looked at her iPhone again and moved on.

'And – one, two, three, four, five down and one, two left – here is Van Kampen.'

Alex looked at the grave. Unlike the painter's tomb it was completely plain except for a beautifully carved number. Of course, thought Alex: of course he wouldn't have any decoration. The tombstone seemed appropriately grim.

Alex crouched down and touched the surface of the stone, worn smooth by centuries of worshippers and visitors. It felt cold – even colder than he thought it would.

'Is he actually under there?' asked Alex.

'Oh yes,' said Angelien. 'He's under there all right. What's left of him anyway.'

Alex was reminded of the tomb with the worm-ravaged corpse and shuddered. He had a sudden realisation that this stone floor concealed a great layer of dead bodies, sleeping under their stone blankets.

'And this,' said Angelien, 'is Hanna's.'

Alex started at the name and felt as though he was standing at the edge of her grave pit, teetering on the brink of falling.

The tombstone was plain save for a design, as on her father's grave, that Alex realised was the first letters of her name. The only other detail was a crisply inscribed number forty-five at the top. Alex was trying to think why that number had some significance, when he recalled that it was the number of his room back at the hotel.

This realisation brought on the dizziness he had felt when looking at the painting of her. The more he looked at the stone, the more he felt like a great darkness was closing in on him. When Angelien spoke, her voice seemed to come from miles away.

'Alex?' she said. 'Alex?'

'What?'

She chuckled.

'I was asking if you wanted to buy any postcards?'

'Oh, right. Maybe.'

'I'll go and see what they have,' she said, walking away.

As soon as Angelien was gone, Alex staggered outside, gasping for air. A group of tourists on a guided tour looked at him suspiciously as he walked to the canal edge and took some deep breaths. The sky had darkened over the church and the building looked black and forbidding.

Alex tried to regain his composure. He felt as if some of the darkness of that grave pit was still clinging to him. He wasn't able to make sense of his feelings and didn't feel ready to share them.

Angelien came out looking for him and he concentrated on taking a photograph even though his hands were still shaking.

'Alex?' she said. 'Are you OK?'

'Me?' he said. 'Yeah. Sure. I just wanted some more photos of the outside.'

Alex took another photograph of the roof against the slate-grey clouds. He was feeling better already.

Angelien took Alex by the arm again and they set off past the pointed turrets of De Waag and on towards the Singel canal. They walked past the university and the mass of bicycles parked beside it. Groups of students were gathered eating sandwiches and laughing beside the canal.

Eventually they crossed a bridge and came to the Bloemenmarkt, a floating flower market on the Singel canal.

The sun came out briefly from between the clouds to light up the colours of the flowers on display and Angelien seemed in a brighter mood to match.

'I'm sorry I got so cross with you,' said Angelien. 'Earlier. I have a terrible temper, like I said.'

'No,' said Alex. 'My fault.'

Alex did not really care about that now. It seemed like it had happened days before. He was happy just to enjoy the glimpse of sunshine and not let his mind dwell on how he had felt in the Oude Kerk. But he knew somehow that wherever he went in this city, he would be pulled back to the mask and to Hanna and to whatever dark mystery lurked behind them.

'In the old days,' said Angelien, 'the growers used to sail up here and moor their boats to sell their flowers. It still floats, but it's a permanent place now. There's something sad about that. I like the idea of all those boats filled with flowers heading up the canals and then disappearing again. Much more romantic, huh?'

Alex nodded.

The shops were full of all kinds of flowers in plastic buckets. Alex hardly knew what any of them were apart from the sunflowers and tulips – there were lots of different types of tulip.

'These are lovely,' said Angelien, leaning forward to inspect some delicate red and yellow ones, whose petals curled to a twisted point like flames.

Without really thinking, Alex picked up a bunch and handed them to Angelien.

'To say sorry for being so much trouble,' he said. 'And to say thank you.'

'You already said sorry,' said Angelien with a smile.

Alex shrugged again.

'This is prettier though,' he said. 'How much are they?'

'You look a little worried,' said Angelien, laughing.

'N . . . No,' said Alex. 'I've got plenty of money.'

'You're sure?' she said.

'Sure,' said Alex.

'Then thank you,' she said.

The woman at the counter wrapped them in brown paper and tied them with a red ribbon. She said a few words in Dutch to Angelien and then chuckled to herself. Alex paid for the flowers and they set off back to his hotel.

'Thanks again for the flowers. It was sweet of you,' Angelien said as she left him at the hotel.

'Nah,' said Alex. 'That's OK.'

Alex stood and watched her walk away along the canal and over the bridge; watched until she had disappeared from view. Then he stood a moment or two more.

12

Alex and his father made their way along the side of a wide, tree-lined canal, the evening sky a chemical green, the street lights just starting to glow. They were making their way to Saskia's house. She had invited them over for a meal.

'You've been very quiet,' said Alex's father. There was a private view going on in a gallery as they passed by. The windows were flung open and the voices of the guests drifted out into the night in a long murmur interwoven with laughter and the clink of glasses.

'I'm OK,' said Alex.

'What did you get up to today?' asked his father.

'Not that much,' he said. 'We went to the Oude Kerk.'

'Did you now?' said his father. 'It's pretty amazing, isn't it? All those tombstones.'

Alex nodded.

Alex was about to tell his father that they had seen Van Kampen's tombstone, when he changed his mind. He knew that once he started, he would end up telling his father the whole story and he didn't want to do that.

The story was so bound up with Angelien that it had become too private, too intimate to share with anyone but her. He hadn't been able to tell her everything but he knew that she was the only person he could tell.

'Of course, you must have seen the red light district too,' said Alex's father, raising his eyebrows. 'What did you make of that?'

'It's really tacky,' said Alex.

His father smiled.

'You seem very relaxed about it,' said his father.

'All ports are a bit sleazy, aren't they?' said Alex casually.

His father chuckled.

'I suppose they are,' he said.

'I've decided what I'm going to write about for my essay,' said Alex.

'Yes?' said his father.

'Yeah,' said Alex. 'I'm going to write about our hotel and how it was in the seventeenth century.'

'Oh, really?' said his father.

'Angelien will help me,' he said. 'She's been

looking at the diary of a painter who lived opposite and –'

'OK, OK,' said his father. 'As long as it's your work and not Angelien's, huh? Ah, here we are.'

They had arrived outside a canal-side house. A small flight of steps with dark railings led to a deep-green door with a small window at the top, divided up into a fan of triangular panels. A large metal doorknocker in the shape of an eagle hung in the centre of the door, but Alex's father pressed a bell push on the wall.

'Jeremy!' said Saskia when she opened the door. 'And Alex. Come in, come in. At least it wasn't raining when you walked round.'

Alex stepped across the threshold and into the house, astonished at how big it was.

'Mum's loaded,' said Angelien seeing the look on his face. 'Everyone thinks she is just a poor little editor, but she only works there because she loves it. She has never needed to work – it's her business after all.'

'Hers?' said Alex.

'Her father was very rich and she was an only child. He started that publishing house in the 1960s. She owns the place – well fifty-one per cent of the shares anyway.'

Alex looked at Saskia, trying to make this adjustment in his head. He had never realised the

135

publishing house belonged to her. His father hadn't said anything that even hinted at it.

'So does that mean you're rich too?' said Alex, looking back at Angelien.

Angelien laughed.

'Do I seem more interesting all of a sudden?' she said. 'Maybe if I bump her off. She doesn't let me think the money is mine. And that's cool. I would not have studied so hard if I had thought that I was just going to get what I wanted without any effort.'

'Don't stand there in the hallway, Angelien!' called Saskia. 'Bring Alex in and get him a drink of something.'

'What do you want, Alex?' said Angelien as they walked into a large, high-ceilinged room lined with books all around. It opened out on to another room just as large with a table already laid for the meal.

'I'm OK thanks,' said Alex.

'How about you, Jeremy?' said Angelien. 'There's a bottle of wine open . . .'

'Wine would be good,' said Alex's father standing in front of a bookcase and taking a book down.

'Do *Androids Dream of Electric Sheep?*' said Alex's father. 'Philip K. Dick? I didn't see you as a sci-fi reader, Saskia.'

Saskia walked forward from the kitchen and stood in the doorway.

'You bought that for me,' she said with a smile. 'A long, long time ago.'

'Really?' said Alex's father, opening the book and reading the inscription. 'So I did. Good Lord.'

'You were so excited about it,' said Saskia. 'You had stayed up all night reading it and the next day you bought me my own copy and said that I simply had to read it.' Saskia chuckled at the memory. 'You were so passionate about everything. It is what first –'

'What was I thinking of?' interrupted Alex's father with a snort. 'Absolute tosh.'

He put the book back and Alex saw the smile fade on Saskia's face as she returned to her cooking. Angelien bit her lip and Alex frowned at his father, who returned to the bookshelves muttering disapprovingly.

'Angelien,' called Saskia. 'Could you give me a hand? It's almost done.'

Angelien got up slowly, looking back at Alex's father, and walked through to the kitchen. Alex could hear them talking in hushed voices, before Angelien called them to the table.

Saskia had cooked them roast pork. She said she knew how men liked their meat and winked at Alex, who got the impression that she was already just a little tipsy.

The food was good and they laughed and talked in the glow of candlelight, although Alex sensed that Saskia wasn't as cheerful as she pretended to be.

The evening went quickly and Alex was surprised at how early it seemed when his father looked at his watch and said they probably ought to be going.

Alex walked to the door with Angelien, leaving his father and Saskia behind in the lounge.

'See you tomorrow then, Alex,' said Angelien.

'Yeah,' said Alex.

'It sounds as though my services may not be needed soon,' she said.

'What?' said Alex.

'Yes,' said Saskia walking up behind them. 'The meetings are almost done and your father will be free to spend a little more time with you.'

'More time?' said Alex's father. 'We haven't really spent *any* time together yet, have we, Alex?'

Alex looked at Angelien and back to his father.

'That's OK, Dad,' he said.

Angelien looked away, out into the night.

'Well, goodnight,' said Alex's father. 'Thanks for the meal. It was a lovely evening.'

'Our pleasure,' said Saskia.

'The first of many I hope,' Alex's father said.

'Goodnight, Alex,' said Saskia.

'Goodnight, Saskia,' said Alex quietly. 'Thanks. Goodnight, Angelien.'

Angelien smiled at him and then turned and went back inside. Saskia waved to them as they walked away. Alex turned back when they had walked a little way, but the door was already closed.

'You like Saskia, don't you?' said his father.

'Yeah,' said Alex. 'She seems nice.'

'Good,' said his father. 'She is. Nice, I mean.'

They walked back to their hotel, the nightlife of Amsterdam in full spate. They picked up their keys from the reception desk and climbed the stairs to their room, saying goodnight in the corridor outside.

Alex could scarcely stay awake long enough to brush his teeth. He collapsed into bed and fell asleep in an instant.

Alex woke suddenly. The room was dark apart from the glow of the street lights behind the curtains. He had heard a noise but wasn't quite sure what it was or where it had come from. He wondered if he had made it himself while asleep. He hoped he had.

His eyes quickly became adjusted to the gloom and he scanned the room looking for something while at the same time hoping he would find nothing at all. It was the same crippling sense of fear again, but the familiarity changed nothing nor did it diminish the intensity of it.

The room was not very large and, being uncluttered, it was the work of seconds to determine that there was nothing in the room but he himself. And yet he felt compelled to check again – and again, even though he knew he would find nothing there. He could see he was alone, and yet that was not enough to stem the dread. Was he going mad? Was this what madness felt like?

Alex got up and walked over to the chest of drawers. The mask was on top again, as though waiting for him. Again the floor seemed to shift beneath him as though a trapdoor had been triggered.

He knew without question that his father hadn't moved it this time. He desperately wanted to cling to the hope of some rational explanation, but there was none.

He picked it up. He felt the chill of it seep into his fingers. He walked to the window and pulled aside the heavy curtain. The canal and street outside looked unremarkable. A fine drizzle had made mirrors of the cobbles and they reflected the lights of the street lamps and shops.

Alex looked down at the mask and then back out at the view. He felt his heartbeat race at the thought of putting it on again. But there was a kind of excitement mixed with the fear.

Alex lifted the mask. He knew that he shouldn't put it on, and yet he also knew that this was just what he was going to do.

He put it to his face and peered through the eyeholes. Once again the overwhelming impression was of darkness – a darkness that seemed to override that of the night. It was a darkness of the mind as much as it was a lack of light.

All the myriad points of light that only seconds before had illuminated the wet streets had now been extinguished, replaced by shifting levels of gloom.

Slowly, discernible shapes began to emerge from this black miasma. It was as though Alex was swimming through the deep, deep ocean, holding his breath and searching the dark waters for danger.

As before, all trace of the present had evaporated, and in its place was the cold and blue-black past, shimmering expectantly like a dark thought.

Alex could hear the strange echo of his own breath, muffled by the mask he held to his face and stifled by trepidation.

Then the children came as before, running and jumping. He could hear their twittering voices and the sound of their shoes and boots upon the cobbles and stone slabs.

His breaths came in faltering gasps. He knew now that he was seeing what Hanna had seen and if *she* saw ghosts then that is what he now saw.

And he knew now that it was true. He could see it in the horrible pallor of their skin – like something dug from under the ground, all pale and lifeless. He saw it too in the hollow of their cheeks and the dullness of their sunken, shadowed eyes.

He wished he was dreaming but he knew he wasn't. If it was a dream he might wake up. He wished he could.

But he did not wake. He couldn't even close his eyes against the vision he was seeing. The girl's will was stronger than his. Because she chose to look, whilst he wore the mask, it seemed as though he must look also.

He could feel his brain revving like an engine forced uphill. His head seemed to be getting hotter and hotter, his breaths shorter, and then all at once the floor opened up beneath him and he dropped.

As he fell, he dropped the mask and the effect was almost instantaneous. Air flooded back into his lungs and he gasped like a man released from a noose.

13

Alex stared at the food on his plate at breakfast, leaving it untouched. His father asked him if he would like to come into the office with him and see what was going on.

'No,' said Alex. 'It's OK.'

'You're sure?' said his father. 'Everything OK?'

'I'm just tired,' said Alex.

His father smiled.

'To be honest,' said his father. 'It's really not that interesting. I just thought you might want a break from Angelien.'

'It's OK,' said Alex matter-of-factly. 'I already texted her. We're meeting here a bit later.'

Alex's father nodded. 'But you're sure everything is all right?'

'Yes!' hissed Alex.

'OK then,' said his father curtly. 'It's just that you seem a bit –'

'I'm *fine*,' he said. 'I'm completely fine.'

His father nodded and took a sip of coffee.

'Well then,' he said. 'I'd better get going. Stay and finish your breakfast.'

Alex's father got up, dropping his napkin on to the table, and left Alex in the café.

Alex sat staring into the distance. Today he had to tell Angelien what he had seen. He had to find some way of making her listen without thinking he was crazy or, worse, some kind of childish fantasist.

The important thing, he decided, was not to just blurt it all out. That really would sound crazy. He needed to take his time and tell her calmly and sensibly.

Angelien texted ten minutes later to say she was in the hotel lobby, and Alex grabbed his jacket and bag and went out to meet her.

'I thought we might go to the Van Gogh museum today,' said Angelien as they left the hotel. 'What do you think? Do you like Van Gogh?'

'Yeah,' said Alex. 'I mean I haven't seen that much. I'm not sure I've seen any real ones.'

'OK then,' said Angelien. 'Then we should definitely go. It's my favourite museum in Amsterdam. Let's have a coffee first though, huh? Have you had breakfast?'

Angelien took him to a café where she ordered

coffee and croissants. 'I used to come to this café when I was a kid, with my dad,' said Angelien. 'It still looks exactly the same.'

Alex watched through the window as a cat curled up on the bonnet of a car on the opposite side of the road. He suddenly felt very tired.

'It will all work out fine,' said Angelien with a smile. 'Believe me.'

Alex smiled. He wanted to believe her.

Several times as they walked along after leaving the café, Alex was about to tell Angelien about looking through the mask, but each time he found that the words would not come. It was going to sound stupid, however he started. He wasn't going to get very far before she laughed in his face.

He was sure that she would think he was dreaming or even making it up. Whichever, he was sure that she would think he was being childish and he didn't want that. He really did not want that.

Besides, he was less and less sure of what he had seen as the morning drew on. Was it impossible that he had dreamt the whole thing? It seemed more comforting to think that he had.

'I read some more of Graaf's journal last night,' said Angelien.

'Yeah?' said Alex.

'It seems like she used to sit in the window of the

house, day after day, looking out at the street. Kids in the neighbourhood would run past when they got to that stretch of the canal or avoid that street entirely. They would dare each other to look at her masked face.'

Alex frowned, imagining Hanna, day after day, the relentless ticking of the clock, the airless room, the window, and her silhouette against it, staring out across the canal, the sound of running feet in the street outside.

'And she never left the house?' said Alex.

Angelien shook her head.

'Never?' he said.

'Doesn't seem like it,' said Angelien. 'And it seems – not surprisingly – as though her time spent holed up in that house had driven her a bit crazy. All that talk of seeing the ghosts of plague children . . .'

Alex turned away and looked towards the canal. Leaves were drifting by on its sepia waters. He had to say something. He had to tell her that he had seen those ghost children himself.

But even as he thought this he was full of doubts: was he seeing the past or was he seeing the madness of Hanna's damaged mind? Was he dreaming? Maybe he was the crazy one.

Then Alex heard footsteps and when he looked round, Dirk was walking towards them, grinning. There was something lupine about his face.

'What's *he* doing here?' said Alex coldly.

'Nice to see you too,' said Dirk.

'You said he wouldn't be coming along any more,' said Alex.

Dirk put his arm round Alex and clutched his shoulder, his fingers digging into him. He made it look friendly but Alex could tell it was meant to hurt and it did.

'You won't tell, will you, Alex?' he said.

Alex shrugged him away.

'Get lost!' said Alex.

'OK, tough guy,' he said.

'Shut up, Dirk,' said Angelien.

'I'm not scared of you,' said Alex unconvincingly.

'You should really be quiet,' said Dirk. 'I don't like bullies. They are usually cowards, you know.'

'You would know,' said Alex.

'Me?' said Dirk with a shrug. 'No. I'm not a bully, my friend. I don't hassle girls with emails and Facebook and so on. It makes me sick, actually – cyber-bullying. That really is a coward's way, huh? They should be a lot stricter with people who do that kind of thing . . .'

Alex stared at Angelien and she put her hands to her face and cursed under her breath.

'What?' said Dirk, laughing.

Angelien looked at Alex but he could see by her

expression that she really had said that. She turned angrily to Dirk and slapped him in the stomach with the back of her hand.

'Hey!' he said with a laugh. 'You said you were sick of babysitting. You said it wasn't worth the money your mother was paying you and –'

'Dirk,' she hissed and turned to Alex, reaching out towards him.

'She's paying you to look after me?' said Alex.

'I know how it sounds,' said Angelien. 'But –'

'I don't care,' said Alex. 'You said I'd change my mind about you when I got to know you better. You're right. You are weird. Weird and –'

'Alex.'

'Leave me alone.'

He shook his head and, ignoring the shouts behind him, walked away over the bridge, tears filling his eyes.

Alex had been walking for a few minutes when a hand tapped him on the shoulder. He turned expecting to see Angelien but was instead faced by Dirk. He saw Alex's reaction and put his hands up and backed away a little.

'It's OK, man,' he said. 'Look, I'm sorry, OK? I acted like an idiot. Angelien told me to come and say sorry.'

'OK, so you said it,' said Alex, turning away and starting to walk off.

Dirk stepped around and in front of him blocking his way. Alex stopped and stared back at him coldly. Behind him further down the road, he could see Angelien waiting.

'Hey,' he said. 'Come on. I've said sorry.'

Alex bit on his bottom lip. He felt sure that it was only Angelien watching that prevented Dirk from grabbing him by the throat.

'Look,' he said. 'I just want to get back to my hotel.'

Dirk smiled.

'Then you're heading in the wrong direction, my friend.'

Alex didn't reply.

'Come on,' said Dirk, stepping a little closer. 'We can be cool about this, huh? Angelien thinks you will go to your dad and get her into trouble again. But I said you wouldn't do that.'

'Why's that?'

'Because you like Angelien,' he said with a smile. 'And you won't want to get her in trouble.'

He felt sick. Angelien had told Dirk everything. Alex imagined them in a café together laughing about him. He felt like Dirk had reached into his chest and was squeezing his heart.

Dirk leaned closer and dropped his voice.

'I don't want to hear that Angelien's witch of a

mother knows about this,' he whispered. 'Don't make me come looking for you, OK?'

Angelien slowly walked towards them.

Dirk slapped him on the back.

'Cool!' he said loudly. 'You're OK, my friend.'

'Everything OK, boys?' she said.

'Sure,' said Dirk. 'Alex is cool. Aren't you, Alex?'

'Yeah,' he said.

Angelien looked relieved.

'So where shall we go next?' she said. 'Dirk was just going and –'

'Actually I think I'm just going to head back to the hotel,' said Alex.

'Really?' said Angelien. 'We'll walk you back.'

'Nah,' said Alex. 'I've got a map. I'll be fine.'

'But –' began Angelien.

'You heard the man,' said Dirk, grabbing hold of Angelien. 'He's fine. He's not a baby. He can find his way back to the hotel without you, can't you, Alex?'

When they had left him, Alex took out his map. Initially he had every intention of returning to the hotel, but as he walked he found that he was being irresistibly drawn in another direction.

Alex walked on, head bowed, staring at the cobbles, his feet seeming to have a will of their own.

Every step he took reminded him of Dirk's

sneering face and the bitterness he felt ran through his whole body like a disease. He ached with it.

All of a sudden Alex stopped. When he looked up, he found himself outside of a shop. He looked in through the window and saw that it was filled with rolls of fabric, multi-coloured buttons and spools of thread.

Alex opened the door, pinging a bell. The woman serving in the shop seemed surprised to see a teenage boy when she looked up but she smiled and said hello.

Alex smiled back and headed to the back of the shop. He seemed to know exactly why he was there and what it was he needed.

In front of him were spools of ribbons in dozens of different colours.

'English?' said the woman stepping up beside him.

'Yes,' said Alex.

'Can I help you?'

'Yes,' said Alex. 'Can I have some of that ribbon – the dark-blue one?'

14

Back in his hotel room, Alex picked up the mask and threaded the ribbon through the holes at the sides, knotting them.

He did these actions mechanically. The bitterness he had felt about Angelien and Dirk had turned to numbness. He felt nothing. He just knew that he had to do this and do it now.

Alex put the mask up to his face and, with some difficulty, tied the ribbon in a bow at the back of his head. It felt cool against his skin, like plunging his face in cold water.

He was startled by what a difference this made to the feel of the mask. Holding it in front of his face had been strange enough, given the weird effect it had on whatever was viewed through it.

But actually tying the mask on made it seem as though it belonged there, as though it was made for him. It fitted his face perfectly, almost as if it was adapting itself to Alex's features. The shape hugged his face and settled coolly across his nose and cheeks and forehead until he could hardly tell where his flesh ended and the mask began.

The view through the eyeholes was as dark as ever, although the time it took to adjust to the difference seemed less somehow and he was definitely seeing more now.

The room was no longer his hotel room, but the room that Hanna had spent her life in. It was sparsely furnished and Alex had the impression that the darkness was not wholly down to the mask. A single lamp provided all the light and its glow barely reached the far side of the room.

Alex walked across to the window and pulled aside the curtain – not the bland curtain of his hotel room, but a heavy damask curtain. Again he heard the echo of his own short breathing. Was it Hanna? Was it her breath that echoed with his own?

Alex looked out through the window and saw the children standing in a group below, all staring up at him as though they had been waiting for him to come to the window.

He let the curtain fall back across the window, blocking them out. But the memory of their faces lingered in his mind.

Alex walked backwards away from the window,

the heavy curtain still swaying slightly, pulling the mask off as he did so. Light flooded back into his sight, dazzling him and making him blink.

He put the mask down on the top of the chest of drawers and stared at it. The face seemed to look back at him, with its inscrutable smile. It seemed to mock him. Alex sat down on the bed and put his head in his hands.

Alex heard his father come into the room next door and got unsteadily to his feet. He opened a drawer and slid the mask inside and then went over to the adjoining door.

'Hi,' he said as he opened it.

'Alex,' said his father, looking up from the papers in his lap. 'I thought you were still out with Angelien.'

'Nah,' said Alex. 'She had to be somewhere so I came back.'

'Hope you haven't had to hang around for too long,' said his father. 'Saskia had a meeting, so it looks like we are both at a loose end. How about we go and eat, just the two of us?'

Alex smiled.

'Yeah,' he said. 'That'd be good.'

They went to a restaurant on the banks of a small, straight stretch of canal, lined with trees with a humpback bridge nearby, crowned with a tiara of bicycles chained to its railing. A garland of lights echoed the curve of the bridge and they reflected in the water, forming a near circle.

'Everything's going to be fine you know,' said his father as they waited for the waiter to bring their food. 'It all seems like it's overwhelming now, but it will pass.'

'I suppose so,' said Alex.

'I'm so sorry that we did this to you,' he said. 'Your mother and me. It was the last thing I wanted, you know that – but I couldn't make your mother stay.'

'I just wish . . .'

But Alex was not really sure what he wished for any more, except for everything to be back to normal.

'I like it being just us two,' said Alex. 'I like Saskia and everything. It's not that.'

His father smiled.

'I'm glad you like her,' he said. 'I'm pretty fond of her myself. We just met at the wrong time. We were too young.'

'Will you marry Saskia, Dad?' asked Alex.

'Marry?' said his father, pouring himself some wine. 'Where did that come from? I think we are a long way off making that kind of decision.'

'It's just that she lives here in Amsterdam,' said Alex. 'Her job's here. Her whole life is here.'

'Alex, Alex,' said his father. 'I don't want you

worrying yourself about all this. Who knows what might happen in the future? Let's talk about something else. What did you do today?'

'Nothing much,' said Alex, remembering Dirk's grip on his shoulder.

'Everything OK?' said his father. 'I shouldn't have gone on at you about Angelien.'

'No,' said Alex. 'You were right. I was being stupid. Of course she wouldn't be interested in me.'

'Well,' said his father. 'Never mind, eh? No harm done. How about pudding?'

Alex felt in no hurry to return to his room and was happy when his father suggested that they walk off their meal by wandering along the canals in a meandering stroll back to their hotel.

The tick-tock of his father's brogues echoed along the dark streets and canals and Alex felt lulled and calmed. Perhaps his father was right: perhaps everything would be fine in time.

This attempt at optimism lasted right up until he said goodnight to his father and found himself alone in his room once more. Within seconds of closing the door, Alex felt the chill eating into the pit of his stomach.

He turned back to open the door and return to his father, but the darkness already had a hold of him. Instead he reached for the chest of drawers.

He knew that the mask was calling to him again. He knew he was not going to be able to resist; he didn't want to resist.

Alex couldn't stop now, he knew it. He had to find out more. He was hooked now and could no more resist the mask than stop breathing. This was not about proving anything to Angelien; this was a raw compulsion. Alex just needed to look into that world. As frightening as it was, he needed to see more.

Alex picked up the mask and tied it quickly round his head, knotting it at the back. It felt tight at first but within seconds he barely noticed it was there. Darkness descended once more, and all the modern trappings of the room fled at its arrival.

He walked across to the window. Resisting all impulses to look down at those pale blue children, he looked straight ahead into the darkness of the houses on the opposite side of the street.

He let those houses shift out of focus and he focused instead on his reflection in the window. It was a dull and vague reflection but he found that, with concentration, he could make the image clearer and sharper.

The mask stood out pale against the blackness behind, but the eyes that twinkled in the shadows of the eye holes were not hazel like his own, but pale and limpid. The flaxen hair that tumbled down on either side was likewise not his own, but Hanna's.

And as he realised that he could see her, he could feel that she made the same realisation. Across the centuries they made contact.

Alex's hands moved up behind his head, but it was Hanna who moved them. It was her fingers that now worked at the knot he had tied in the ribbon.

Alex's heartbeat quickened as he realised what was happening. She was taking the mask from her face; a face that Angelien had said was horribly disfigured in the fire. He braced himself.

Then suddenly, he saw a black shape loom up behind Hanna's face. It was Van Kampen appearing like a huge crow. He stopped Hanna's fingers as she tried to untie the bow, looking out into the street, clearly concerned at who might be watching.

Hanna pulled away from his touch and walked away from the window. Alex could feel her temper rising. Van Kampen turned and began to walk away but Hanna called after him. Alex couldn't understand what she said but he could see through her eyes the effect it had on her father. He staggered backwards as though shot and put his hands over his ears.

She shouted again, louder this time. Hanna's father turned and walked back to his room and though Alex was relieved, the relief was short lived, because Van Kampen strode back, his cane high over his head.

Without pause or warning the cane cracked across Hanna's back. Hanna curled up to shield herself against the next blow, but it came too quickly. Alex felt the pain that Hanna felt and it was almost too much to bear.

Hanna screamed as the next blow came down and Alex cried out too. He turned to see a look of wild fury on Van Kampen's ashen face: fury, tinged with a kind of terror. He was lashing out at them as someone might strike out at a snake or a rat.

The cane came down again and cracked, the handle breaking off and skittering across the floor. Van Kampen raised the broken cane above his head and Alex cried out again. Another blow from the cane knocked the mask from Hanna's face and sent it bouncing across the floor.

As soon as the mask came off, the modern world flooded back in. He heard his father's footsteps approaching the door and he leaped back into bed, shoving the mask under the covers.

'Alex!' said his father walking in and turning on the light. 'I heard you scream. What's the matter?!'

Alex was still disorientated. The past world of Hanna still clung to him. He tried to speak but a wordless sound emerged. His father's voice sounded distant and faint.

'Alex!' repeated his father.

This time the voice rushed in through the haze, like a wave crashing on to a fog-bound shingle beach. The world of the mask fled from the light, reality reappearing, crisp and sharp. Alex felt as though he had been slapped awake from a deep sleep.

'Alex,' said his father, more quietly this time, putting his arm round his son's shoulders. 'What's wrong?'

'The mask,' said Alex. 'I had a nightmare. A bad one.'

'That bloody mask,' said his father. 'It's an ugly thing if you ask me. There's something unpleasant about it. If Angelien thinks it's worth so much, then why not give the thing to her.'

'No!' said Alex, more aggressively than he intended. 'I want to keep it, Dad.'

His father sighed. 'What was the nightmare about?' he asked. 'It sometimes helps to talk about these things, you know.'

'It was about this house,' said Alex. 'About the way it was in the Golden Age, you know, when Van Kampen lived here with his daughter.'

'He had a daughter, did he?' said Alex's father. 'I suppose Angelien has been telling you all this.'

'Yes,' said Alex. 'The girl used to wear a mask like

the one I bought. I suppose it must have creeped me out a bit.'

His father stroked Alex's hair and stood up.

'I'm OK, Dad,' said Alex.

'Sure?' he said, standing up.

Alex nodded.

'OK then,' said his father. 'If you're sure. Stop thinking about the seventeenth century. It's a gloomy age. Try and concentrate on something cheerful.'

'Like World War Two?' said Alex.

'Ha!' said his father. 'Fair point. Just try and get some sleep, son. Goodnight.'

Alex's father walked through the connecting doors, closing them behind him. As soon as he had gone, Alex kicked the mask out from under the duvet and, without looking at it, turned over and closed his eyes.

15

Alex sat on his bed watching the BBC news on his television, without really taking any of it in. He was still in a daze from the night before. He was dimly aware of the sounds of the street drifting in through the window and now and then he heard the tread of other guests. His father knocked and opened the door.

'You're sure you don't want any breakfast?'

Alex shook his head.

'I feel bad leaving you here,' said his father. 'Maybe it's better if you come with me.'

Alex could hear that his father didn't really believe that. Alex was sure that his father dreaded the idea. What if Alex caused some sort of scene at the publishers?

'It's all right, Dad,' he said. 'Go. I'm OK.'

'If you need anything,' said his dad, 'just call.'

His father had made him promise to stay in his room. He said he probably wouldn't be back by lunchtime and if Alex got hungry he could ring room service.

Alex lay on his bed. Every time he closed his eyes he saw Van Kampen lurching forward with his cane. No one was going to believe him, least of all his dad.

He could have told everything to Angelien but he was scared that she would think he was just a stupid kid. He could bear his dad thinking he was crazy, but he couldn't bear that.

Alex read his book fitfully, breaking off every now and then to mull over some episode from the last few days. By twelve he was starting to regret not having breakfast when the phone next to his bed suddenly rang, sounding startlingly loud. He was unsure what to do at first but thought that it might be his father calling from reception and so crawled across the bed and answered it.

'Hello?' he said.

'Alex?' said a voice at the other end he recognised straight away.

'Angelien?' said Alex coldly. 'What do you want?'

'I'm in reception,' said Angelien. 'Come and get me. I tried texting you but your phone is off.'

'I know,' said Alex. 'I switched it off.'

There was a long silence.

'Come on, Alex,' she said. 'You're angry with me, I know. But I need to talk to you.'

Alex took a deep breath.

'Why?' said Alex. 'I thought you only talked to me if you got paid.'

'Come on,' she said. 'The manager is giving me a funny look. Don't leave me here. It's about Hanna.'

'OK,' said Alex after a pause. 'I'll come down.'

Alex walked down the stairs, getting more agitated with each step. He was in the grip of a confusing mix of anger, hurt and a kind of nervous exhaustion.

Angelien was sitting at a table by the window as he walked past the reception desk. He walked over and sat down opposite her, looking out at the canal.

'I read some more of Graaf's journals last night,' she said.

'What?' said Alex. 'That's it? I don't even get a sorry or anything?'

Angelien slumped back in her seat.

'I'm sorry, Alex,' she said. 'Really.'

'Why did you have to tell him about what I said?'

Angelien shrugged.

'Because that's what people do when they go out with each other, Alex,' she said. 'They talk about things. I had no idea Dirk was going to say anything to you. It was wrong of him. He can be a jerk sometimes.'

'Sometimes?' said Alex shaking his head.

'Look,' said Angelien. 'I get enough of this from my mother, OK? Let's just forget about Dirk, huh? Do you want to know what I've found out or not? I thought you'd be interested.'

Alex stared at her for a few moments sullenly, and then nodded.

'Come on,' she said. 'Let's go get a coffee.'

'I don't know,' said Alex. 'I kind of promised Dad . . .'

'OK,' said Angelien. 'I don't want to get you into trouble. But there's a place just at the end of the street. You look like you could do with some fresh air. Have you eaten?'

'No,' said Alex. 'I'm starving.'

'Well come on then,' said Angelien.

Alex nodded and he opened the door for her to walk through, the cold, damp air sweeping over them as they exited the hotel.

'Wait till you hear what I have to say,' she said.

'I'm not really sure I should talk to you about the mask and stuff any more,' said Alex without looking at her. 'My dad says –'

'Hanna wasn't burnt as a baby,' said Angelien. 'Hanna's face wasn't burned at all.'

'Then why did she wear the mask?' said Alex.

Angelien shrugged.

'The painter wondered if Van Kampen did it

because of what happened with his wife. Maybe he was punishing his daughter because he couldn't punish his wife. Maybe he was stopping her from going out so that she would never leave him.'

'But why make her wear a mask?' asked Alex.

'Maybe because her mother had run away with a man, Van Kampen was trying to hide her face from view – from any possible suitor in the future.'

'But that's crazy,' said Alex.

'Hey,' said Angelien. 'All men are crazy as far as I'm concerned. Van Kampen certainly told the painter that his daughter's face was horribly burned. Maybe Van Kampen had told her that too, from when she was little. Maybe she even believed it. He did not allow mirrors or even polished surfaces in the house. Only Van Kampen saw her with the mask removed. The servants weren't allowed to take it off.'

'But surely she would have taken it off herself,' said Alex. 'In all those years. She must have felt her own face and realised it was fine. Wait . . . Maybe that's why he beat her.'

'Beat her?' said Angelien. 'What do you mean? What makes you think he beat her?'

'I just . . . I don't know,' said Alex. 'How did Graaf know all this anyway? If Van Kampen never let anyone see, how did Graaf know it was a lie?'

'The painter was there when she died,' said Angelien.

He knew that Hanna was dead – of course he knew that she was dead – but still those words seemed to explode inside Alex's head. He had shared his mind with Hanna – shared a body with her. He had become so bound up entirely in her story that hearing of her death seemed like a bereavement.

'Alex?' said Angelien.

'Yeah,' he murmured. 'I was just . . . How did she die?' He thought of the beating again and felt the crack of the cane on his ribs. 'Did Van Kampen kill her?'

'Van Kampen?' said Angelien, frowning. 'No. Well not directly anyway. I suppose you could argue that his treatment of her was to blame . . .'

'For what?' said Alex.

'She climbed out of her bedroom window and threw herself down on to the street.'

They both looked down at the cobbles in the street where she must have landed. Alex thought of the beckoning children and shuddered.

'Come on,' she said. 'Let's go get a coffee.'

After a moment's hesitation, Alex nodded.

'Graaf saw the commotion and ran round to Van Kampen's house,' Angelien said as they walked. 'He arrived only moments after she had jumped. She was already dead. Someone removed her mask and Graaf saw her face for the first time, her pale eyes open and staring up at the sky. Is this place OK for you? We can sit outside.'

'OK,' said Alex, pulling up a metal chair as a waitress came out. Angelien ordered and then returned to her story.

'Hanna had landed on her back and her face was untouched by the fall. It had no sign of burning at all and far from being hideously deformed by fire, Graaf described her as very beautiful.'

Alex shook his head. Van Kampen was a vicious creep. It was all his fault. He had driven her to it. 'Her father might as well just have shoved her out of the window!' Alex said.

'You sound very angry about Hanna's story, Alex,' said Angelien.

But it didn't feel like a story to Alex. Each time he put the mask on, Alex felt more of Hanna's darkness seeping into his soul. He was not entirely sure where his feelings ended and hers began.

'That's what I love about history,' said Angelien. 'The way you can get caught up –'

'No,' said Alex. 'It's more than that.'

Alex leaned back in his chair.

'Oh?' she said.

Alex paused for a long time, trying to find the right words to start.

'The mask,' said Alex. 'The one I bought in the antiques market. It's kind of haunted.'

Angelien sighed.

'Alex,' she said. 'Are you joking with me?'

'It's true. I swear. When I look through it, I can see what Hanna saw. I saw the ghosts of the plague children. When I wear it, I am kind of half me and half Hanna. It's hard to explain.'

Angelien looked at him for a little while and then spluttered into laughter.

'It's true,' said Alex. 'You have to believe me.'

'I'm sorry, Alex,' said Angelien. 'But this is too crazy.'

'But you said you thought anything was possible the other day.'

'Hey, Alex,' said Angelien. 'I try to have an open mind, but not a weak mind, huh? Come on. This is too silly.'

'You're lying,' said Alex. 'You were as obsessed with Hanna's story as I was, you know you were.'

'I'm a historian, Alex,' said Angelien. 'We get carried away sometimes.'

'I don't believe you,' said Alex. 'There was more to it than that. You know there was. I didn't even know about the painting when I bought the mask. And what about all the other stuff – the hotel key rings and –'

'We don't even know the mask is the same one as in the painting, Alex.'

'I do,' said Alex.

Angelien sighed.

'Even if it was,' she said, 'That doesn't make it magic or haunted. There may be a thousand masks like that – but there could be a logical explanation for all this.'

'Like what?' said Alex in exasperation.

'Calm down, Alex,' said Angelien. 'Have you told your dad about any of this?'

'No,' said Alex. 'He'd think I was crazy. I thought you'd be different.'

Angelien took a deep breath and smiled. She leaned forward, putting her hands on either side of his face.

'I'm sorry,' she said. 'Really.'

Alex felt like everything was sliding away and he needed to do something fast. He had to stop talking and do something.

Alex lunged forward, putting his hand behind her head and kissing her on the lips. Angelien pulled herself away and stood up, knocking her chair over.

'What the hell –' she said angrily, glaring at him.

Alex stared at her. That was not the reaction he had hoped for.

'What have we here?' said a voice Alex already knew too well.

'What?' he said, turning to look at Dirk and then staring back at Angelien. 'What's he doing here?'

Angelien rattled off a volley of Dutch. Dirk just laughed and wagged his finger in admonishment.

'English, Angelien,' he chided. 'Think of the little boy here.'

'Shut up!' yelled Alex, getting to his feet.

'Whoa!' said Dirk holding his hands up. 'Don't get so worked up, my friend. You'll hurt yourself.'

Alex swung a punch at Dirk that took him by surprise, hitting him in the ribs and making him wince. He grabbed Alex by the throat and pushed him towards the canal.

Angelien shouted something at Dirk in Dutch.

'What the hell is going on?' said Alex's father suddenly appearing with Saskia, heading back to the hotel.

'Angelien?' said Saskia.

Dirk let go of Alex, smirked and backed away.

'Get away from my son!' hissed Alex's father, jabbing his finger at Dirk.

'Jeremy,' said Angelien. 'I'm so s—'

'And you can stay away from him as well!' growled Alex's father.

'Hey! Don't talk to her like that,' said Alex.

Alex's father turned towards him with an expression he had never seen before. He took a step back.

'What did you say?'

'Leave her alone,' said Alex more falteringly.

Alex's father peered at him incredulously.

'You think she cares about you?' said his father. 'For God's sake, Alex. Wake up! Look at her. She's laughing at you, Alex. She just wants to get stoned with scum like him.'

'Hey!' said Angelien.

Dirk stifled a laugh.

'I don't think I like the way you are talking about my daughter,' said Saskia.

'Oh well I'm very sorry,' said Alex's father. 'We mustn't say anything bad about your precious daughter, must we?'

'You need to calm down, Jeremy,' said Saskia. 'Let's all just –'

'Perhaps if you were a bit harder on her she wouldn't dress like she works in the red light district and hang around with druggy pieces of –'

'That's enough!' shouted Saskia. 'How dare you? Who do you think you are?'

Alex saw his father open his mouth to speak but

the words never came. Everyone was looking at him, even a passer-by who was pretending to talk on his mobile phone.

'We are finished at the office,' said Saskia coolly. 'And I think that so are you and I, Jeremy. If you need anything more, you can contact my secretary.'

'Saskia . . .' he said. 'Saskia!'

But she was already walking away and she didn't look back.

'Angelien!' she called without turning round, and after a moment, Angelien followed after her. Dirk shook his head, smirking, and walked off in the opposite direction.

Alex's father stood there looking up at the glowering sky. He closed his eyes and Alex prepared himself for a tirade but it never came. His father just opened his eyes, looked at him for a moment and then set off for the hotel. Alex stood for a while in the deserted street and then set off after him.

16

For a long time, Alex and his father didn't talk at all. Then gradually they found a functional meeting place of single words and shrugs. His father tried to book them on a flight back that evening but there was nothing until the following morning. They settled down in their respective rooms to while away the time.

It seemed ridiculous to be in a city like Amsterdam and spend the last day in a hotel room, but Alex accepted it as unavoidable under the circumstances. He could hear his father tapping away at his laptop in the next room as he looked out of the window at yet another rain shower.

What was for sure was that things would never be the same again back home. Alex felt as though he saw things more clearly now.

Alex picked up his mobile and sent a message to his mother. It read simply, *Sorry*. He knew now how much he must have hurt her. He hoped she would understand.

Alex vowed that when he got back to England he would go and see his mother and talk about everything. He would tell her about Molly and Angelien and Hanna and the mask.

Alex switched on the television and flicked through the channels, failing to find anything he wanted to watch. He picked up his book and began to read, but he just didn't feel able to concentrate. He lay back on his bed and stared at the ceiling. The muffled sound of the outside world and his father's tapping faded away and he closed his eyes and fell asleep.

It felt like only seconds later when he woke with a start, but when he looked at the clock by his bed he could see it was over an hour later. The day was drifting slowly towards twilight. He stretched and sat up.

Alex went to the bathroom and poured himself a glass of water and drank it in one go. His mouth still felt dry. He looked in the bathroom mirror and he almost didn't recognise himself. The trials of the last couple of days seemed etched on to his face.

What a mess it all was. He had come to Amsterdam hoping to put the troubles at home and at school behind him, but he had simply swapped those troubles for new ones.

One thing was for sure, the mask was staying in Amsterdam. He might not be able to solve everything, but at least he could leave Hanna and Van Kampen behind. He had enough troubles of his own to deal with without getting caught up in things that happened centuries ago.

Walking back into the bedroom, Alex went over to the chest of drawers. He would put the mask in the bin and that would be that. But on opening the top drawer he was surprised that the mask wasn't there.

Then he remembered that it was still under the bed. Alex dropped to his knees and looked and bent forward, pressing his face to the carpet and peering into the gloom. There, like a skull in a grave pit, was the mask, smiling, deathly pale.

Alex froze. Tears sprang to his eyes. He knew now that he looked at it, that he shouldn't touch it – that he would pack his clothes and leave it be for the cleaners to find. But he also knew in that instant that he couldn't stop himself.

Alex stretched out his arm and grabbed the mask. As always, the surface felt cold, and its chill had seeped into his flesh.

Alex tied the mask on and looked around the room. The change was expected now. Even the fact that daylight was extinguished didn't surprise him any more.

Alex again had the feeling that there were two people inside his head. Or was it that he had invaded the head of the girl? Did she have the same strange sensation as him?

Some time had elapsed since the beating. He could still feel the pain that Hanna carried from it, but it was an ache now. But her anger was still raw. Alex could feel it burning cold, like ice.

He walked over to the window and, pulling aside the curtain, looked out at the canal. It was that more-than-night of Hanna's world. The plague children were already gathered in the street outside.

They moved into a huddle below the window. They had their heads bowed, as though deep in thought, but they seemed to know that Hanna was at the window because they all, as one, raised their pale-blue faces and stared up.

Then, one by one, the ghostly children raised their thin blue-white arms and beckoned, their skinny fingers curling and uncurling as though they were trying to coax a bird from a tree.

They were beckoning to Hanna. They were willing her to come and play with them; to free herself from her father's captivity and run in the streets with them.

Death was the price to be paid for this freedom

and Alex could already feel the part of him that was Hanna agreeing that this price was worth paying. She would join them soon enough.

Hanna turned and walked across to the connecting door to her fathers' room. Alex felt his own arm reach out but it was Hanna's hand that appeared in his field of sight, edging towards the latch of the door to the adjoining room. It was not the white-painted door of his hotel room, but the dull, dark one of Hanna's world.

He felt his hand – her hand – close around the latch. He felt the smooth chill of its touch on the palm. He heard the faintest click of the latch and the whisper of the door brushing slowly open.

Through the widening crack he saw that the room was not the room his father slept in. There was instead a much darker, gloomier chamber, sparsely furnished and dominated by a tall four-poster bed, hung all about with heavy curtains.

Van Kampen was in that bed, behind those curtains. He could hear his sleeping breaths, rasping rhythmically like the clock in his room.

His terror of Van Kampen waking was almost unbearable. Alex desperately wanted to go back to his room and to his own time, but Hanna's will was stronger.

Their tread was soundless and the girl's bare feet

walked ever so gently across the wooden floor. She had a lightness he could never have achieved.

Alex could sense her wariness and his own fear returned as he realised she was worried that her father might wake up. She walked past the end of the bed and towards a table near the window on which stood a glass and a wine decanter and a smaller, dark-green bottle.

Alex knew that she would reach for that small bottle. He knew too that she would remove the stopper from the wine decanter. He felt the glass stopper and the weight of it as she pulled it out and set it noiselessly down on the table top.

The small green bottle contained a fine white powder and he watched as the girl's hand carefully lifted it, tipping some of the contents into the wine with practised precision. She had done this before and more than once.

She looked at the powder dissolving in the wine for a moment and then carefully put the bottles back exactly as she had found them. Alex wondered if it was poison but knew Van Kampen would hardly leave poison sitting next to his wine. More likely it was some kind of medicine. Whatever it was, he knew that Hanna meant him harm.

Why should he care? He hated his father. No. It was Hanna who hated her father. Her mind was melting into his. He struggled to keep track of his own thoughts.

Van Kampen moved in his sleep but did not wake. But it was a sign to get moving. As noiselessly as they had entered the room, they now left, closing the door silently behind them. Hanna's power over him seemed momentarily weakened by her fear that her father would wake and Alex reached up and took the mask off.

He threw it on the bed and adjusted his eyes to the light. Even though it was a gloomy afternoon, it seemed dazzlingly bright after the darkness of Hanna's world.

Alex looked round to face the connecting doors. He could hear his father still tapping at his laptop. A few minutes later he opened the door and asked Alex what he wanted to eat.

They ordered food and ate it in Alex's father's room in near silence. His father said that Alex could watch a movie if he wanted to but that he was going to get some work done and then turn in.

Hanna had been trying to kill her father, Alex was sure of it. Maybe she succeeded. Alex couldn't imagine that he could ever be angry enough with his father that he would want him dead, let alone be the cause of his death. But then his father had not beaten him the way Van Kampen had beaten Hanna.

Alex felt complicit somehow. Even though he hadn't willed it, he still felt as though his hand had poured that powder into Van Kampen's glass. Could he have resisted? Could he have stopped Hanna?

17

When Alex woke, he was standing at the window wearing the mask. For a moment he thought he was dreaming, but only for a moment.

He tried to put his hands to his face to remove the mask, but they would not obey him. He was back in Hanna's world and it was she who was in control here.

The canal outside was once more as it was in the painting. Hanna looked straight ahead into the darkness and again Alex could see her eyes twinkle in the curved eyeholes in the reflected mask. He felt her face form a hidden smile that mirrored the frozen smile of the mask and Alex felt his face compelled to do the same.

Hanna's scarred hand reached up to the window latch and opened it. The chill night air rushed in.

Alex knew what she was doing and yet was powerless to stop himself mirroring her actions as she stepped up on to the windowsill and leaned out to look at the ghost children way below.

Hanna teetered there on the sill, between standing and falling, between life and death. The moment seemed to go on for ever. Alex tried to resist. If he jumped with Hanna, was he jumping in his own time? If he died here, would he join Hanna and those ghostly children? He summoned up every last ounce of his dwindling will and yelled.

'No!'

As the sound of his voice died away, Alex felt his will fade along with it. He looked down with Hanna at the spectral faces below.

'Alex!'

Alex's grip on the window frame loosened. He was already falling when his father grabbed his arm and pulled him inside, falling as he did so and dragging his son on top of him. They lay together on the floor, Alex's father holding him tightly.

His father got up and went to the window and closed it. He pulled the mask from Alex's face, tossed it to the ground and stamped on it, splitting it into pieces.

Alex's father looked at Alex with an expression of bewilderment.

'Alex,' he said breathlessly. 'What . . . Why were you . . .'

'I'm sorry, Dad,' said Alex, sobbing. 'I'm sorry.'

'You looked like you were going to . . .' began his father.

Alex's father hugged him and they sat together on the bed. Alex looked down at the broken mask and knew that the spell that went with it was broken too. He did not know whether Hanna was now free of this place or whether Alex was simply free of her influence, but something had changed, he could feel it.

'Alex,' said his father. 'Why? I don't understand . . . Is this about Molly Ryman?'

Alex shook his head.

'About your mum and me?'

'I can't explain it, Dad,' said Alex.

'Try.'

'You wouldn't believe me,' said Alex. 'I wanted to tell you about the mask before . . .'

His father shook his head and groaned.

'Please tell me this isn't about that damned mask?' said his father. 'For God's sake, Alex. You were about to . . .'

Alex struggled to concentrate. Noises seemed to rush forward like angry bees, buzzing around his head before disappearing in a background hum. His head hurt and he sat on his bed while his father fetched him a glass of water.

'Talk to me,' said his father. 'Please.'

'You won't believe me,' said Alex.

'Alex,' said his father with a sigh. 'Just tell me.'

So Alex told him some of what had happened over the last few days. He told him about the mask and about the painting. He told him about Angelien's research into the house and the painter's journal. He told him about seeing Hanna's reflection when they first arrived and how he had felt haunted by a presence in the room the whole time they had been there.

Alex's father listened attentively and without once interrupting. At first Alex was pleased that he was being allowed to get his words out, but the more it went on, the more self-conscious he became and the less sure of what his father was thinking.

When he had reached the end of his story, his father lowered his head, closed his eyes and rubbed them with his finger and thumb, as he always did when he was searching for the right words. When he raised his head, Alex was shocked to see tears in his eyes.

'Dad?' said Alex.

'Alex,' said his father. 'I'm so sorry. This is all my fault. I haven't appreciated how stressed you have been by everything that has gone on,' continued his father. 'Your mother leaving was a big blow, I know that.'

'What's that got to do with this?' said Alex, frowning.

'Look, Alex,' said his father reaching out and putting a hand on his knee. 'You're a very intelligent boy. But you're also a . . . sensitive boy.'

'What's that supposed to mean?' he said.

'Alex,' said his father gently. 'The business at school? You aren't coping very well, are you? The business with the Ryman girl and now . . .'

'This has got nothing to do with what happened at school!' said Alex.

'Do you remember the nightmares you had when Mum left?'

Alex took a deep breath before answering.

'This wasn't like that,' said Alex.

'Wasn't it?' said his father.

'You haven't listened to anything I've said. You never listen.'

Alex's father put his hands to his face and rubbed his eyebrows.

'Alex,' he said quietly. 'I have listened to you. That's why I'm concerned. That's why –'

'I shouldn't have told you,' said Alex.

'Of course you should,' said his father. 'Please try and –'

'I'm tired, Dad,' said Alex. 'I'm going to get to sleep.'

Alex's father looked at the floor for a while.

'OK,' he said. 'I'll see you in the morning. You're sure you'll be all right? You can come in here with me.'

Alex smiled weakly.

'I'll be fine. Honest.'

'OK,' said his father. 'But any problem, Alex, and just come through to me.'

His father looked at the window.

'I'm very annoyed with Angelien for encouraging all this . . .'

Alex could see that he was going to say 'nonsense'.

'It's nothing to do with Angelien,' said Alex. 'She thinks I'm crazy too, if you must know.'

'So you've told her about this?' said his father.

'Not much,' said Alex. 'Only a bit.'

Alex's father covered his face with his hands again.

'What are we going to do with you, Alex? Angelien must have told Saskia. I thought she was being strange with me –'

'Saskia is cheesed off with you because you don't listen to her either,' said Alex angrily. 'And you made fun of that book of hers.'

'What book?' said his father. 'What are you talking about, Alex?'

'Never mind,' said Alex. 'What's the point?' Alex's father closed his eyes and let out a long slow breath.

Eventually he reached out and laid his hand gently on Alex's shoulder.

'I'm OK, Dad,' said Alex, knowing what was on his mind. His father nodded.

'Get some sleep,' he said. 'Everything always seems much clearer in the morning.'

After a few moments Alex nodded.

'Yeah,' he said, without much conviction.

18

There was a calmness now that Alex realised contrasted sharply with the pent-up atmosphere which had existed for the whole of his stay in that room. It was as if a storm had broken and cleared the air.

He was sure that somehow Hanna – or the ghost of Hanna – had been freed by the destruction of the mask. She had left the room – left the hotel, Alex was sure of that. Trapped in life and in death, she was finally liberated.

Alex too felt freed. His senses seemed keener, where before all but his sense of fear had been muffled. He felt older too, as though he had aged years in a single day.

The broken mask lay in the waste-paper bin of his hotel room and no longer held him in thrall. Its hold over him was as broken as the mask itself.

'The place has been freezing the whole stay,' said

his father, tapping the air conditioning. 'Now it's boiling all of a sudden.'

Alex picked up his bag. They were all gone now, he thought: Hanna, Van Kampen, the plague children too. Their spirits had moved on to who knew where.

Down in the lobby his father handed their keys back and asked about the bill.

'No, no,' said the manager with a smile. 'Everything has been taken care of. I hope you have enjoyed your stay.'

'We've been very comfortable, thank you,' said Alex's father.

The manager looked across to Alex and smiled.

'I have something for you,' he said. 'Your young lady friend left this for you.'

Alex walked across to the counter and the manager gave him an envelope, ignoring the cold stare of his father.

'Thank you,' he said.

'Would you like me to call you a taxi, sir?' said the manager.

'That won't be necessary, thank you,' said Alex's father. He said that they would catch the train to Schiphol and also said that they would walk to the station.

It was as if he didn't want to spend another second

longer in the hotel than necessary, even to wait for a cab.

Alex didn't care how they got home, he just wanted to get there with as little fuss as possible.

Even school seemed attractive now – despite all the trouble and the dark looks and sniggers; its familiarity was appealing and he felt that it now held little fear for him.

Picking up their bags, they walked to the door and out into the street. Alex looked back at the window of his room, just as he had done when they had first arrived. The sun was shining now and the windowpane borrowed the blue of the sky. Alex had no impression of a hidden presence behind that reflection.

Alex had half expected to see Angelien, but the street was empty save for the bicycle traffic crossing the nearby bridge. He would never see Angelien again, he knew that.

He thought he heard a voice call his name and turned to the sound. There was nothing there: nothing but a movement in the waters of the canal – shoals of light flickering and shimmering on the surface.

Alex followed his father along the street and over the bridge, heading for Damrak, the long boulevard that led to the central station.

Damrak was heaving with people, moving back and forth along the wide pavements while trams zipped along the street. Every single person on the long street seemed to be a tourist, either walking to the centre from the station or walking, like them, to catch a train out of the city.

The central station was a big, grand building with frescos on the outside and domes on the roof. They walked past the rows of tram stops towards the entrance.

They bought tickets from a machine, Alex's father searching his pockets for the right coins. Alex stood impassively nearby as a couple embraced passionately before separating with tearful goodbyes.

They travelled upstairs in the train, sitting opposite an elderly couple who clutched their bags to their breasts as though they suspected Alex was going to snatch them at any moment. Alex put on his iPod and looked out of the window.

The train was taking them back alongside the motorway they had driven along with Saskia and Angelien on their journey into the city, and that brought back images of Angelien. A flickering slide show flashed by of the time he had spent with her. These images were like barbs that pulled painfully on his mind. He now saw his relationship with Angelien as his father must have seen it; as Saskia must have seen it; as Angelien must have seen it. His mind flinched at each new thought.

How could he have ever thought that someone like Angelien would be interested in a boy like him? What a joke. What a big fat joke.

At the airport, they bought some sandwiches and sat on stools in view of the departures board. Their flight was yet to be assigned a gate number and a flashing sign told them to wait.

Alex took out his phone. There was a message from his mother. *That's OK, Alex. Whenever you're ready.*

'Come on,' said his father, picking up his bag. 'That's our gate.'

Alex followed after him and they retraced their steps from the beginning of their journey to board their plane.

Alex stowed his bag, took a seat next to the window and put his book in the string pocket at the back of the seat in front. He doubted if he would be able to concentrate enough to read it. His father was already reading his book, ignoring Alex and the cabin crew, who were beginning their safety drill.

Minutes later they were airborne and heading out over the sea. The day was another dark and dismal one and the sea looked almost black below. Within moments they were surrounded by grey cloud.

Alex glanced round at his father, who he could see was utterly engrossed in his book. He had folded Angelien's letter up and put it in his jacket pocket. He had been waiting for a chance to read it, and could not wait any longer. He took it out now as unobtrusively as possible and unfolded it.

Dear Alex

I am so sorry that things have worked out the way they have. I wanted to come and say goodbye but I promised my mother I would stay away. You probably would not have wanted to see me anyway, huh?

I wanted to share with you the last piece of the puzzle about Hanna. I know that you will want to know – however angry you are with me.

I've read the last part of Graaf's journal and we've been wrong the whole time. Hanna was not driven mad by wearing that mask – although I'm sure it did not help.

The painter couldn't stop thinking about Hanna and her story. Even after she died he still was obsessed with her. He took the mask home with him and hung it in his studio while he painted the picture we saw in the Rijksmuseum. He went to Van Kampen's home in Utrecht and talked to people who knew them there – to the servants who used to work in the house before his wife ran away.

At first he could find nothing new, but then he met a man who used to work for Van Kampen and he discovered something amazing. That man seemed pretty sure that Hanna had started the fire at the house when she was a little girl.

He said that Hanna was always a strange child but she became even stranger when her father came back with a mask from Japan.

Van Kampen had laughed when she had first put it on, but then Hanna insisted on wearing it all the time. Her mother was expecting another child and Hanna went berserk when she found out. She followed her mother about, watching everything she did, staring at her through the mask. The mother became terrified of the girl – terrified of her own daughter.

And it seems like she had good reason because there was a fire in the mother's bedroom one evening when she was resting. Hanna was the only person about and she was burnt by the fire. At first it seemed as though she had heroically tried to save her mother, but her mother said that she had woken to see the girl moving slowly around the room spreading the fire.

Hanna's father would hear none of it. She could do no wrong in his eyes and he seemed convinced that the mother was mistaken. The mother had a miscarriage and as soon as she recuperated she ran away and was never seen again.

We have been imagining that her father was an evil man, but maybe he was just misguided. Maybe he thought he could keep his daughter safe by locking her away. Or keep her from doing harm. He must have known deep down how troubled she was.

It seems that Hanna was not the poor imprisoned girl we thought she was. Although Hanna was burnt in the fire, the burns were restricted to her hands. She chose to wear the mask all the time and her father told the story of her burns to try to explain it.

Back in Amsterdam, Graaf discovered through a servant of Van Kampen's that the day before Hanna jumped to her death she had heard the girl taunting her father, telling him how she had started the fire back in Utrecht and how she wished she had killed her mother and the unborn child. Her father flew into a rage and beat her with his cane until finally it broke in two.

That night, Van Kampen died in his sleep. People said that he had died of a broken heart, but Van Kampen's physician told Graaf of his suspicion that the real reason was probably an overdose of a sleeping draught he had been prescribed.

Perhaps keeping the truth about Hanna from the world just became too much for him. Perhaps he did die of a broken heart after all.

It was Hanna who discovered him dead and jumped from the window. Perhaps she really did love him in her way. Or maybe she just realised that, however much of a half-life she had endured, she had no life without him.

Goodbye, Alex, and sorry. I never meant for you to get hurt. I hope everything works out for you back in England. Don't hate me.

Angelien

Alex stared out of the window into the darkness. He remembered walking through to Hanna's father's room. He remembered how Hanna had poured the sleeping draught into his wine. Van Kampen did not commit suicide. Hanna killed him before she jumped.

Alex was sure that, whatever Angelien thought, there was something evil about that mask and he was glad he was rid of it.

The plane had touched down and was coming to a halt. Alex looked out of the window at the bright lights of the terminal gleaming in the murk. He was returning to Angelien's letter when his father leaned over.

199

'What's that?' he asked.

'Nothing,' said Alex, folding it up and putting it in his pocket.

His father said nothing more, just closed his book and stood up to get their bags down. All through the plane, all the passengers were doing the same.

They caught the shuttle train to the main terminal and queued up at UK passport control. Alex was tired. All the disturbed nights and stress of the last few days was finally taking its toll. He ached and longed for his own bed.

Alex and his father headed for the exit marked *Short Stay Car Park*. Alex looked at the dark figure of his father ahead, hunched and somehow smaller. Rain had begun to fall. Arc lights lit up the wet car roofs and windscreens. The roar of aircraft engines rent the sky.

Alex's father paid for the parking ticket and headed for their car, which was parked a little way off. They seemed to be the only people in the whole car park.

The lights blinked and the locks answered the call of the key with an electronic chirrup. Alex put his bag in the boot and his father slammed it shut. Alex chose to sit in the back of the car and his father started the engine and pulled out of the parking space, following the maze-like route of arrows to the exit barriers.

Once out on to the road they headed for the M11, the traffic building slowly with each junction. Eventually they were on the motorway and heading south to London.

Alex reached into his pocket and took out his iPod, squeezing the ear buds into his ears and switching it on. A long, rhythmic introduction started up – a simple bass line, then drums, then guitars. He tried to place it but couldn't and didn't bother to check.

He sank back into his seat as they overtook an articulated lorry, the spray from its tyres washing over them. The headlights of the oncoming cars flickered through the barrier of the central reservation.

Alex happened to glance at the rear-view mirror in passing. Something caught his eye and he looked again. There was something black: something black sitting in the reflection near to where he was sitting. It was like a shadow but a shadow of something that was not there.

He felt as though the car had suddenly crested a hill. His stomach lurched and his heart seemed to falter in its beating and judder like meat slapped down on a butcher's counter.

Try as he might to insist to himself that there was nothing there, the blackness at the edge of his vision was too real, too potent to ignore or wish away. He leaned sideways and stared into the rear-view mirror.

Instead of his own face looking back, it was the face of Hanna, the pale skin glowing from the shadows. The lights of a passing truck lit up her face for a moment and made her pale eyes sparkle.

Alex wanted to cry out. He wanted to shout to his father, but Hanna placed her fingers to her lips in the mirror and Alex was quiet.

He looked across at his bag lying on the seat next to him and dragged it on to his lap. He pulled it open and there, staring back undamaged, whole once more, was the mask.

READ ON FOR A TASTER OF
ANOTHER SPINE-TINGLING TALE
FROM THE MASTER OF THE MACABRE

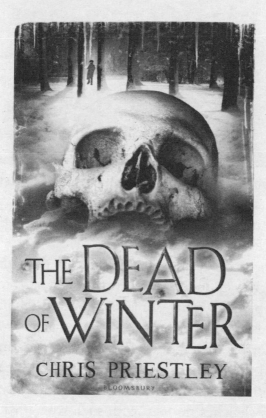

'Deliciously creepy with lots of twists and turns'
Daily Mail

PROLOGUE

My name is Michael: Michael Vyner. I'm going to tell you something of my life and of the strange events that have brought me to where I now sit, pen in hand, my heartbeat hastening at their recollection.

I hope that in the writing down of these things I will grow to understand my own story a little better and perhaps bring some comforting light to the still-dark, whispering recesses of my memory.

Horrors loom out of those shadows and my mind recoils at their approach. My God, I can still see that face – that terrible face. Those eyes! My hand clenches my pen with such strength I fear it will snap under the strain. It will take every ounce of willpower I possess to tell this tale. But tell it I must.

I had already known much hardship in my early years, but I had never before seen the horrible blackness of a soul purged of all that is good, shaped by resentment and hatred into something utterly vile and loveless. I had never known evil.

The story I am to recount may seem like the product of some fevered imagination, but the truth is the truth and all I can do is set it down as best I can, within the limits of my ability, and ask that you read it with an open mind.

If, after that, you turn away in disbelief, then I can do naught but smile and wish you well – and wish, too, that I could as easily free myself of the terrifying spectres that haunt the events I am about to relate.

So come with me now. We will walk back through time, and as the fog of the passing years rolls away we will find ourselves among the chill and weathered headstones of a large and well-stocked cemetery.

All about us are stone angels, granite obelisks and marble urns. A sleeping stone lion guards the grave of an old soldier, a praying angel that of a beloved child. Everywhere there are the inscriptions of remembrance, of love curdled into grief.

Grand tombs and mausoleums line a curving cobbled roadway, shaded beneath tall cypress trees. A hearse stands nearby, its black-plumed horses growing impatient. It is December and the air is as damp and cold as the graves beneath our feet. The morning mist is yet to clear. Fallen leaves still litter the cobbles.

A blackbird sings gaily, oblivious to the macabre surroundings, the sound ringing round the silent cemetery, sharp and sweet in the misty vagueness. Jackdaws fly overhead and seem to call back in answer. Some way off, a new grave coldly gapes and the tiny group of mourners are walking away, leaving a boy standing alone.

The boy has cried so much over the last few days that he thinks his tears must surely have dried up for ever. Yet, as he stares down at that awful wooden box in its frightful pit, the tears come again.

There are fewer things sadder than a poorly attended funeral. When that funeral is in honour of a dear and beloved mother, then that sadness is all the more sharply felt and bitter-tasting.

As I am certain by now you have guessed, the lonesome boy by that open grave is none other than the narrator of this story.

CHAPTER ONE

I looked into that grave with as much sense of dread and despair as if I had been staring into my own. Everything I loved was in that hateful wooden box below me. I was alone now: utterly alone.

I had never known my father. He was killed when I was but a baby, one of many whose lives were ended fighting for the British Empire in the bitter dust of Afghanistan. I had no extended family. My mother and I had been everything to each other.

But my mother had never been strong, though she had borne her hardships with great courage. She endured her illness with the same fortitude. But courage is not always enough.

These thoughts and many others taunted me beside that grave. I half considered leaping in and joining her. It seemed preferable to the dark and thorny path that lay ahead of me.

As I stood poised at the pit's edge, I heard footsteps behind me and turned to see my mother's lawyer, Mr Bentley, walking towards me accompanied by a tall, smart and expensively-dressed man. I had, of course, noticed him during the funeral and wondered who he might be. His face was long and pale, his nose large but sharply sculpted. It was a face made for the serious and mournful expression it now wore.

'Michael,' said Bentley, 'this is Mr Jerwood.'

'Master Vyner,' said the man, touching the brim of his hat. 'If I might have a quiet word.'

Bentley left us alone, endeavouring to walk backwards and stumbling over a tombstone as he rejoined his wife, who had been standing at a respectful distance. Looking at Jerwood again, I thought I recognised him.

'I'm sorry, sir,' I said, gulping back sobs and hastily brushing the tears from my cheeks. 'But do I know you?'

'We have met, Michael,' he replied, 'but you will undoubtedly have been too young to remember. May I call you Michael?' I made no reply and he smiled a half-smile, taking my silence for assent.

'Excellent. In short, Michael, you do not know me, but I know you very well.'

'Are you a friend of my mother's, sir?' I asked, puzzled at who this stranger could possibly be.

'Alas no,' he said, glancing quickly towards the grave and then back to me. 'Though I did meet your mother on several occasions, I could not say we were friends. In fact, I could not say with all honesty that your mother actually liked me. Rather, I should have to confess – if I were pressed by a judge in a court of law – that your mother actively *dis*liked me. Not that I ever let that in any way influence me in my dealings with her, and I would happily state – before the same hypothetical judge – that I held your late mother in the highest esteem.'

The stranger breathed a long sigh at the end of this speech, as if the effort of it had quite exhausted him.

'But I'm sorry, sir,' I said. 'I still do not understand . . .'

'You do not understand who I am,' he said with a smile, shaking his head. 'What a fool. Forgive me.' He removed the glove from his right hand and extended it towards me with a small bow. 'Tristan Jerwood,' he said, 'of Enderby, Pettigrew and

Jerwood. I represent the interests of Sir Stephen Clarendon.'

I made no reply. I had heard this name before, of course. It was Sir Stephen whom my father had died to save in an act of bravery that drew great praise and even made the newspapers.

But I had never been able to take pride in his sacrifice. I felt angry that my father had thrown his life away to preserve that of a man I did not know. This hostility clearly showed in my face. Mr Jerwood's expression became cooler by several degrees.

'You have heard that name, I suspect?' he asked.

'I have, sir,' I replied. 'I know that he helped us after my father died. With money and so forth. I had thought that Sir Stephen might be here himself.'

Jerwood heard – as I had wanted him to hear – the note of reproach in my voice and pursed his lips, sighing a little and looking once again towards the grave.

'Your mother did not like me, Michael, as I have said,' he explained, without looking back. 'She took Sir Stephen's money and help because she had to, for her sake and for yours, but she only ever took the barest minimum of what was offered. She was a very proud woman, Michael. I always respected that. Your mother resented the money – and her need for it – and resented me for being the intermediary. That is why she insisted on employing her own lawyer.'

Here he glanced across at Mr Bentley, who stood waiting for me by the carriage with his wife. I had been staying with the Bentleys in the days leading up to the funeral. I had met him on many occasions before, though only briefly, but they had been kind and generous. My pain was still so raw, however, that even such a tender touch served only to aggravate it.

'She was a fine woman, Michael, and you are a very lucky lad to have had her as a mother.'

Tears sprang instantly to my eyes.

'I do not feel so very lucky now, sir,' I said.

Jerwood put his hand on my shoulder. 'Now, now,' he said quietly. 'Sir Stephen has been through troubled times himself. I do not think this is the right time to speak of them, but I promise you that had they not been of such an extreme nature, he would have been at your side today.'

A tear rolled down my cheek. I shrugged his hand away.

'I thank you for coming, sir – for coming in his place,' I said coolly. I was in no mood to be comforted by some stranger whom, by his own admission, my mother did not like.

Jerwood gave his gloves a little twist as though he were wringing the neck of an imaginary chicken. Then he sighed and gave his own neck a stretch.

'Michael,' he said, 'it is my duty to inform you of some matters concerning your immediate future.'

I had naturally given this much thought myself, with increasingly depressing results. Who was I now? I was some non-person, detached from all family ties, floating free and friendless.

'Sir Stephen is now your legal guardian,' he said.

'But I thought my mother did not care for Sir Stephen or for you,' I said, taken aback a little. 'Why would she have agreed to such a thing?'

'I need not remind you that you have no one else, Michael,' said Jerwood. 'But let me assure you that your mother was in full agreement. She loved you and she knew that whatever her feelings about the matter, this was the best option.'

I looked away. He was right, of course. What choice did I have?

'You are to move schools,' said Jerwood.

'Move schools?' I said. 'Why?'

'Sir Stephen feels that St Barnabas is not quite suitable for the son – the ward, I should say – of a man such as him.'

'But I am happy where I am,' I said stiffly.

Jerwood's mouth rose almost imperceptibly at the corners.

'That is not what I have read in the letters Sir Stephen has received from the headmaster.'

I blushed a little from both embarrassment and anger at this stranger knowing about my personal affairs.

'This could be a new start for you, Michael.'

'I do not want a new start, sir,' I replied.

Jerwood let out a long breath, which rose as mist in front of his face. He turned and looked away.

'Do not fight this,' said Jerwood, as if to the trees. 'Sir Stephen has your best interests at heart, believe me. In any event, he can tell you so himself.' He turned back to face me. 'You are invited to visit him for Christmas. He is expecting you at Hawton Mere tomorrow evening.'

'Tomorrow evening?' I cried in astonishment.

'Yes,' said Jerwood. 'I shall accompany you myself. We shall catch a train from –'

'I won't go!' I snapped.

Jerwood took a deep breath and nodded at

Bentley, who hurried over, rubbing his hands together and looking anxiously from my face to Jerwood's.

'Is everything settled then?' he asked, his nose having ripened to a tomato red in the meantime. 'All is well?'

Bentley was a small and rather stout gentleman who seemed unwilling to accept how stout he was. His clothes were at least one size too small for him and gave him a rather alarming appearance, as if his buttons might fly off at any moment or he himself explode with a loud pop.

This impression of over-inflation, of over-ripeness, was only exacerbated by his perpetually red and perspiring face. And if all that were not enough, Bentley was prone to the most unnerving twitches – twitches that could vary in intensity from a mere tic or spasm to startling convulsions.

'I have informed Master Vyner of the situation regarding his schooling,' said Jerwood, backing away from Bentley a little. He tipped his hat to each of us. 'I have also informed him of his visit to Sir Stephen. I shall bid you farewell. Until tomorrow, gentlemen.'

I felt a wave of misery wash over me as I stood there with the twitching Bentley. A child's fate is always in the hands of others; a child is always so very powerless. But how I envied those children whose fates were held in the loving grip of their parents and not, like mine, guided by the cold and joyless hands of lawyers.

'But see now,' said Bentley, twitching violently. 'There now. Dear me. All will be well. All will be well, you'll see.'

'But I don't want to go,' I said. 'Please, Mr Bentley, could I not spend Christmas with you?'

Bentley twitched and winced.

'Now see here, Michael,' he said. 'This is very hard. Very hard indeed.'

'Sir?' I said, a little concerned at his distress and what might be causing it.

'I'm afraid that much as Mrs Bentley and I would love to have you come and stay with us, we both feel that it is only right that you should accept Sir Stephen's invitation.'

'I see,' I said. I was embarrassed to find myself on the verge of tears again and I looked away so that Bentley might not see my troubled face.

'Now then,' he said, grabbing my arms with both hands and turning me back to face him. 'He is your guardian, Michael. You are the ward of a very wealthy man and your whole life depends upon him. Would you throw that away for one Christmas?'

'Would he?' I asked. 'Would he disown me because I stay with you and not him?'

'I would hope not,' he said. 'But you never know with the rich. I work with them all the time and, let me tell you, they are a rum lot. And if the rich are strange, then the landed gentry are stranger still. You never know what any of them will do . . .'

Bentley came to a halt here, realising he had strayed from the point.

'Go to Hawton Mere for Christmas,' he said quietly. 'That's my advice. That's free advice from a lawyer, Michael. It is as rare and as lovely as a phoenix.'

'No,' I said, refusing to change my grim mood. 'I will not.'

Bentley looked at the ground, rocked back and forth on his heels once or twice, then exhaled noisily.

'I have something for you, my boy. Your dear mother asked me to give this to you when the time came.'

With those words he pulled an envelope from his inside coat pocket and handed it to me. Without asking what it was, I opened it and read the enclosed letter.

Dear Michael,

You know that I have always hated taking anything from that man whose life your dear father saved so nobly at the expense of his own. But though each time I did receive his help it made me all the more aware of my husband's absence and it pained my heart – still I took it, Michael, because of you.

And now, because of you, I write this letter while I still have strength, because I know how proud you are. Michael, it is my wish – my dying wish – that you graciously accept all that Sir Stephen can offer you. Take his money and his opportunities and make something of yourself. Be everything you can. Do this for me, Michael.

As always and for ever,
Your loving mother

I folded the letter up and Bentley handed me a handkerchief for the tears that now filled my eyes. What argument could I have that could triumph against such a letter? It seemed I had no choice.

Bentley put his arm round me. 'There, there,' he said. 'All will be well, all will be well. Hawton Mere has a moat, they tell me. A moat! You shall be like a knight in a castle, eh? A knight!' And at this, he waved his finger about in flamboyant imitation of a sword. 'A moated manor house, eh? Yes, yes. All will be well.'

I dried my tears and exhaustion came over me. Resistance was futile and I had no energy left to pursue my objection.

'Come, my boy,' said Bentley quietly. 'Let us quit this place. The air of the graveyard is full of evil humours – toxic, you know, very toxic indeed. Why, I knew a man who dropped down dead as he walked away from a funeral – dead before he reached his carriage. Quite, quite dead.'

Bentley ushered me towards his carriage and we climbed inside. The carriage creaked forward, the wheels beginning their rumble. I looked out of the window and saw my mother's grave retreat from view, lost among the numberless throng of tombs and headstones.

MISTER CREECHER

'A BRILLIANT COUNTERPOINT TO
FRANKENSTEIN, COMPELLINGLY WRITTEN'
Chris Riddell

'MISTER CREECHER IS A MOST
IMPRESSIVE ACHIEVEMENT'
Guardian

'THIS EXCITING, AFFECTING AND BLOODY
STORY IS A CLEVER TRIBUTE TO AN
ENDURING CLASSIC'
Financial Times

'A BEAUTIFULLY WRITTEN GOTHIC
METAFICTION'
The Times

THE TALES OF TERROR COLLECTION

'Wonderfully macabre and beautifully
crafted horror stories'
Chris Riddell

'Guaranteed to give you nightmares'
Observer

'A delightfully scary book'
Irish Times